HEAD ROCK HARBOR MYSTERY #1

HEAD FOR MURDER

I0544338

CHASE CONNOR

Book Cover Designed By: Chase Connor
©2023 Chase Connor; The Lion Fish Press

Published By:

The Lion Fish Press
539 W. Commerce St #227
Dallas, TX 75208

Chase Connor Books
www.chaseconnor.com

AUTHORS' NOTE:
This is a work of fiction. Names, characters, places, and incidents either are the product of the authors' imagination or are used fictitiously, and any resemblance to actual persons, living or dead, business establishments, events, or locales is entirely coincidental. None of this is real.

E-book ISBN 978-1-951860-47-9
Paperback ISBN 978-1-951860-48-6

Also by Chase Connor

LGBTQ+ YA Books

Just a Dumb Surfer Dude: A Gay Coming-of-Age Tale
Just a Dumb Surfer Dude 2: For the Love of Logan
Just a Dumb Surfer Dude 3: Summer Hearts
A Surplus of Light
GINJUH
When Words Grow Fangs
Sending Love Letters to Animals and Other Totally Normal Human Behaviors

LGBTQ+ New Adult/Lit Fic/MM Romance

The Bees and Other Wild Things (sequel to *A Surplus of Light*)
A Tremendous Amount of Normal
The Gravity of Nothing
Between Enzo & the Universe
The Warmth of Our Closest Star
A Straight Line (w/ co-author J.D. Wade)

LGBTQ+ Magical Realism

Possibly Texas

A Point Worth LGBTQ Paranormal Romances

Jacob Michaels Is Tired (Book 1)
Jacob Michaels Is Not Crazy (Book 2)
Jacob Michaels Is Not Jacob Michaels (Book 3)
Jacob Michaels Is Not Here (Book 4)
Jacob Michaels Is Trouble (Book 5)
CARNAVAL (A Point Worth LGBTQ Paranormal Romance Story)
Jacob Michaels Is Dead (Book 6)
Jacob Michaels Is… The Omnibus Edition (all 6 JMI books and CARNAVAL)

Head Rock Harbor Mystery series

Head for Murder (Book 1)

Erotica

Bully

Briefly Buddies
Jake (A Novella from Tricked: The Men of Briefly Buddies)
Tricked: The Men of Briefly Buddies eBook

Audiobooks

A Surplus of Light: A Gay Coming-of-Age Tale (narrated by Brian Lore Evans)
Between Enzo & the Universe (narrated by Brian Lore Evans; Tantor Media)

Translated

Between Enzo & the Universe – **Spanish**
A Surplus of Light – **Spanish**

Dedicated To:

My family. For forgiving me for all the long hours I spent behind a keyboard and all the true crime and murder mysteries I forced you to watch in the name of research.

To Officer J for answering all of my stupid questions without treating me like I'm stupid.

To Dr. R for answering my medical questions—even the gross ones that had absolutely nothing to do with this book.

Contents

CHAPTER ONE

On Friday, Chief Nelson found a body in the harbor. A *dead* body. Entirely naked, cyanotic, and relatively fresh, it was a morbid start to the day. As if that gossip being whispered amongst the stacks didn't kick up a big enough flurry of excitement in the shop, Rattlesnatches created absolute chaos in the science fiction aisle. Inundated with customers within minutes of flipping the front door sign to 'Open,' I'd absentmindedly left my basket of embroidery skeins on the ledge of the second-floor balcony that overlooks the shop. The morning began crazy and stayed that way until nearly lunch time. While I was distracted helping excited shoppers select their next great weekend read, Rattlesnatches was enthralled with the unattended basket.

Tangled in the loops of thread after batting them around all morning unchecked, Rattlesnatches panicked. With a hiss and a leap, the basket—and my cat—tumbled over the balcony to the shop floor below. Skeins of multi-colored thread rained down upon confused science fiction shoppers, followed by a yowling Abyssinian, claws extended, desperately trying to catch himself. Confusion turned to terror—especially when Rattlesnatches caught himself.

Around the neck of Sawyer Robison.

Two-hundred and thirty pounds of country-boy science fiction geek danced around in panic and pain. Two shelves were toppled. Another teen browsing the science fiction section received three scratches under his right eye from my startled cat. Lila Westbrook—owner and evening front desk clerk at the Head Rock Harbor Inn—was nearly crushed under one of the tumbling shelves. And a pyramid-shaped display of Harrison Garner's latest bestseller was toppled.

When the dust settled and bandages and antiseptic—along with copious apologies—were being doled out to my customers, I looked up to find Rattlesnatches staring down at us regally, unbothered, from the second-floor balcony. His reign of terror, and escape, had been swift. My cat was unbothered, unimpressed, and ultimately, proclaimed not guilty in a court of his own construction.

Fortunately, smalltown folk are forgiving. By the time I had rung up the remaining pre-lunch customers in the store, the incident had mostly been forgotten by all injured parties. Head Rock Harbor isn't New York City. Lawsuits and condemnations are the furthest thing from anyone's mind. So, at noon, on the dot, I set about closing up for my hour-long lunch break.

As a last order of business before stepping away from the shop, I dashed up the stairs, two at a time, to confront Rattlesnatches. The second-floor balcony runs the width of the shop. Halfway along the wall behind the balcony was the door that granted entrance to my tiny efficiency apartment. During work days, I typically leave the door open so that Rattlesnatches won't feel neglected while I'm working.

However, if his behavior didn't improve, that would have to change.

"*You*," I hissed, jabbing an accusatory finger when I breached the top of the stairs.

A wedge-shaped noggin popped up over the arm of the easy chair by the door to my apartment, and a pair of almond shaped coppery eyes assessed me casually. Rattlesnatches' ears flicked up, as if to express shock that I remembered his assault on the bookstore earlier. *How is this guy still upset about that?* As I stood there, fuming, my finger pointing directly at him, Rattlesnatches yawned lazily and rose to sit up and return my stare.

"Do you want to be locked inside all day?" I asked. "Do you?"

The ruddy cat merely stared back at me, his eyes blinking lazily.

Obviously, we had different thoughts on the gravity of him mauling my patrons.

"Because that's what's going to happen," I said. "One more thing. *One more.* And you'll be spending business hours in the apartment. You hear me?"

Rattlesnatches stared at me a moment longer, sniffed the air, then laid down, disappearing behind the arm of the chair. I rolled my eyes and lowered my finger, well aware that chastising him was a lost cause. Rattlesnatches had no remorse. My cat, like all other cats, is a psychopath without the work ethic (or ambition) required to commit actual atrocities, such as murder. So, while uniquely dangerous, cats are all mostly harmless.

I would either have to start locking Rattlesnatches up each day or continue to pray that he would behave himself while customers were in the shop. While locking him up was really the best and safest option, customers of Head Rock Harbor Books would be disappointed. Though Rattlesnatches had gained a reputation for being erratic—and possibly dangerous—customers were actually excited to catch a glimpse of him when they came to the bookstore. Elusive and antisocial—though not particularly mean—seeing my cat during a visit to the bookstore was a special treat for a lot of my customers.

Kids especially squealed with glee if they saw him stalking along the tops of bookshelves or leaping from one shelf to the next. If it was a particularly good day for him, and he laid in his basket in the corner window of the store, customers could gently pet him. Every customer in the store would actually gather around him, offering pets and baby talk. Rattlesnatches pretended to be above it. Even annoyed. But at least twice a week he would take up his post, waiting for the commoners to pay him his dues. It was simply one of the draws of the shop.

From time to time, he was known to actually join me at the check-out counter, sitting regally by the computer as I accepted payments from customers. Everyone delighted in offering head and chin scratches, or the occasional swipe of his back, as they waited for me to bag up their books and print their receipt. Usually, he merely glared down at all of us from the balcony, but it was still a sighting customers could enjoy.

Locking up Rattlesnatches each day was not an option. He knew it and I knew it. With a defeated sigh and a slump of my shoulders, I gave up. Snatching my jacket off of the hook by the apartment door, I left it open when I headed back to the stairs. My descent was less energetic, but I found my way to the front door of the shop.

Lifting the plastic switch cover, I flicked the shop lights off before lowering the cover once more. The switch cover—a small plastic box on hinges—had been installed shortly after I had taken Rattlesnatches in off of the streets. Nothing more than a scroungy, street-smart, and distrusting cat—barely out of the kitten stage—he had quickly figured out how to flip the lights on and off. A little leap with outstretched paws, and he could flip the switch whenever the mood struck him.

Training and admonishments had no effect on Rattlesnatches—as he had shown no capacity for shame—so preventative measures were put into place. A cheap plastic box, two hinges, four screws, and ten minutes of my time were all it took to thwart Rattlesnatches plans. He might have been street-smart, but without the ability to stand on two legs, and with no opposable thumbs, he was no match for the owner of Head Rock Harbor Books. I was no idiot, but simply a bleeding heart for an alley cat with more sass than necessary that needed a home.

I flipped the 'Open' sign to 'Closed' and stepped out onto the sidewalk, letting the door gently click close behind. As usual, I gave the doorhandle a cursory jiggle before turning south to walk down Harbor Street.

I'd barely had time to notice the sparse crowd that was still milling about at the south end of the street, which overlooked the harbor. Gawking at the police cars, caution tape, and the flashing lights produced a flashback to tourist season that sent a shiver up my spine. Nothing like a dead body in the harbor to bring out the rubberneckers.

I did my best to ignore the sight as I strolled passed Charlene's Chocolates, the shop directly south of my bookstore. Charlene herself was stepping out of the chocolate shop for her lunch break, her arms overburdened with a box full of printed flyers and pamphlets. With her arms performing an intricate balancing act, and her mind elsewhere, she nearly plowed right into me.

Ever since she had won the election to become president of the Harbor Street Business Owners Association, Charlene Hardy had been insufferable. Sweet...*but insufferable*. No one took a job—which was more ceremonial than anything—as seriously as Charlene. She failed to acknowledge that she had run in the election unopposed because no one else took the association seriously. Secondly, her goals for the association were loftier than the aspirations of all of the business owners on Harbor Street combined.

I cringed when I saw the box in her arms, knowing I'd return from lunch to find an assortment of the printed materials had been slipped through the mail slot of the bookstore. Hoping Charlene hadn't noticed my reaction, I gave her a smile and made pleasantries as we passed each other, headed in opposite directions. The smell of cinnamon, sugar, and chocolate met my nose as she flounced away, followed by something less pleasant.

Eggs? *Rotten eggs.*

I turned up my nose once our backs were to each other, hoping that whatever had produced the smell hadn't found its way into one of her creations. As much as I didn't adore the woman—though I didn't exactly have strong feelings one way or the other for her—I knew her chocolates to be exquisite. Whatever the smell was, Charlene would have thrown herself from a bridge before letting any of her treats turn out less than spectacular.

A few doors down, I was grabbing the doorhandle of Munchies Café. I'd passed The Loft, a store owned by Ainsley Bucksworth, that sold homewares far beyond the budget I had to decorate my little apartment over my bookstore. Pain had been the next store I'd passed. A bakery owned by Henry Mathis, no one had been able to convince him that the French word for bread was probably not the best word to have emblazoned in capital letters over the door of his bakery. That probably didn't even really work in France. Too on the nose. The breads were excellent, and Henry, like the rest of us business owners on the street, did what he wanted, so it was moot.

It was possible I was planning to stop in Pain for a loaf of Henry's delicious Jalapeno Cheese bread before returning to work. With my mouth watering, I shuffled into Munchies, hoping that a hearty lunch would chase away all of my cravings. It was unlikely, but it was worth a shot. A lifelong love affair with food is rarely resolved by eating. That had been my experience, anyway.

"Jackson!"

My eyes flitted up to find Shirley Templeton waving excitedly at me from the counter at the back of the store where she was helping another customer. I waved back and jerked a questioning thumb at the booth in the front window of the restaurant.

"You go ahead, hon!" Shirley nodded. "I'll be over in a minute."

I slid into the booth seat and slipped a menu from the little holder at the end of the table to peruse, though I already knew what I'd be ordering. I nudged my jacket off of my shoulders, letting it flop onto the seat behind me. I reached up to rub the tip of my nose warm with the palm of my hand right as Shirley materialized at my table. I had begun to massage my nose as she spoke.

"Pork tenderloin. Fries. Ranch for dipping. Slaw," she said, not bothering to jot anything down on her pad. "That about cover it?"

Pretending to be offended was pointless.

"No idea how you do that." I teased her, lowering my hand from my nose to grin impishly.

"It's only your order ninety percent of the time." She slapped at my shoulder.

Shirley jerked her head as she looked up to glance through the picture window the booth was nestled against.

"You hear the news?" she asked.

"Body in the harbor?" I nodded. "Yeah. Folks were talking about it in the shop all morning."

Shirley was still staring out the window, but her head was shaking back and forth slowly.

"Some darn drunken fool probably slipped," she said, her eyes finally trailing back over to me. "It's always this time of year, isn't it?"

Frowning, I said, "A body in the harbor? This is a first."

"You know what I mean." She chuckled lightly. "These folks, tired of being inside all winter. The first not-so-cold evening of spring and they act a fool. Go out. Get drunk. Stumble all over the place. Someone always ends up hurt."

"But not dead." I laughed. "They never get *that* drunk. And it wasn't far above freezing last night."

Shirley sighed. "I suppose it was bound to happen sooner or later. You can only have so many incidents before someone gets hurt for real."

"I guess?" I relented. "Any idea who?"

"Nah." She waved me off, shaking the thoughts from her head. "My bet's on Mavis, though."

"Mavis Attberry?" I barked out a laugh. "Mavis is more likely to hurt someone else."

Shirley cackled. "I know that's about right. But ain't no one drunker than her at the end of the night. You know she shot up the front door of Bernie's Tavern the other night?"

My stare told Shirley all she needed to know.

"Sure did." She nodded firmly. "Went up there after they closed and everyone had gone home and blew a hole straight through the front door with her shotgun. All 'cause they kicked her out for stumblin' around like a fool and botherin' the gentleman customers."

Shirley winked at me. We both knew "gentleman" was an overly polite way to describe Bernie's late-night male customers.

"How's she going to find her sixth husband otherwise?" I asked.

Once again, Shirley was slapping at my shoulder. Without another word, she headed towards the kitchen to put my order in with Lardell, the cook—and also owner—of Munchie's Café. Other than those two titles, Lardell also held the esteemed title of Father of Shirley.

I watched as Shirley shouted my order through the pass to Lardell. Out of sight, his voice rang through the café.

"Hey there, Jackson!"

I chuckled. *"Hey, Lardell!"*

I really needed to get a new lunch routine. My eyes had drifted over to the window to look out onto Harbor Street, but Shirley was at the tableside again before I could get lost in my thoughts. Setting a bowl of coleslaw atop a saucer in front of me, a few packages of crackers tucked in beside the bowl, she was shaking her head down at me.

"Didn't even get a ticket," she said.

"What?"

"Mavis. Marv responded since it was the middle of the night and he lives down by Bernie's, you know?"

I nodded and began to unwrap the paper napkin wrapped silverware Shirley passed to me.

"Marv told her to go home and sleep it off. She shoots up a guy's business and doesn't even get a ticket. How's that for being Chief? Just lettin' ole biddies shoot up other people's businesses and not doin' a darn thing about it."

"Bernie probably didn't want to press charges," I suggested. "He's always had a soft spot for Mavis."

"Marv took her shotgun, though." Shirley smiled widely. "Told her she could get it back when she learned to act right."

"He'll be slipping that gun into her casket when the time comes," I said with a shake of my head.

Shirley and I shared a laugh, and once again, she slipped away.

Reaching up to rub a tickle from my nose, I slid the spoon from the set of silverware, prepared to dig into the bowl of slaw while I waited for my tenderloin. No sooner had I scooped a healthy bite of creamy cabbage from the bowl than someone was sliding into the booth across from me.

"Freeze," Jeremy said. "You're under arrest."

I hadn't had a chance to say anything before he was snatching the two packages of crackers from my saucer. Quickly, I shoveled the bite of slaw into my mouth. Jeremy ignored me as he began ripping open the packages of crackers. If I didn't eat quickly, he'd steal my spoon and my bowl of coleslaw before I could stop him.

"That joke never gets old," I said.

"Not like these crackers." He frowned as he chewed the first bite of his stolen food. "*Shirley! These crackers are stale, darlin'!*"

Shirley, over at the cash register, didn't even look up to respond.

"When you pay for something, I'll let you complain, Germ!"

Jeremy shrugged, stuffed another cracker in his mouth, and chewed vigorously.

"How about some chili?" he asked loudly. "And more crackers? *Fresh ones!*"

"Will do, hon," Shirley responded.

"And put his food on his own ticket," I mumbled.

Shirley cackled. Jeremy glowered at me.

Munchies Café, despite its trendy, cutesy name, is like eating at your grandmother's house. With the rough wood tables and chairs, beaten up booth seats, dark wood-paneled walls, and yellowed linoleum, it's run informally. It's nothing to hear a diner scream an order across the room at Shirley. The café isn't much bigger than a grandma's living room, anyway.

I shoveled my coleslaw into my mouth as quickly as I could, finishing my bowl in record time as Jeremy polished off the crackers he had stolen from me. His nose and cheeks looked as mine felt. Bright pink and chapped, I could tell he had been outside all morning. When he saw me watching him, my mouth full and masticating my last bite of slaw, he grinned and slid the wool cap from his head.

Blond curls fell to his ears before he brushed his fingers through them, pushing them back from his forehead. Between his curls and his pink nose and cheeks, he was practically cherubic. Of course, anyone who knew Jeremy would never compare him to something so angelic.

Satan in a Sunday dress.

That's what my aunt had called him on more than one occasion. She'd have never used the term "cherubic."

"What it do, Jacks?" Jeremy kicked my shin under the table.

Shrugging, I asked, "You been down at the harbor all morning?"

"I'm starving."

"That's not an answer."

"And freezing."

"The harbor?" I asked again.

He waved me off. "Yeah. I was down there all morning. Some drunk guy falls and bashes his head on a rock and dies. Of course, Head Rock Harbor's best detective is on the case."

"Head Rock Harbor's *only* detective."

Jeremy sniffed. "Still the best."

"Fine," I said. "Who was it?"

Jeremy, shrugging his narrow yet muscular shoulders out of his wool peacoat, took his time in responding. He loved delaying my gratification when it came to the gossip around town. He let his coat fall into the booth behind him, then looked over at me again. His tie was slightly askew, his dress shirt ruffled. Perpetually youthfully handsome, the guy didn't even have to try.

"Family hasn't been notified yet," he said, blankly.

I rolled my eyes.

"You're telling me all of those folks standing there watching at the end of Harbor Street haven't seen the body and know who it is already?" I asked. "If you don't tell me, I'll know within seconds of opening the shop after lunch."

"Fair enough," he said. "Prescott Pemberton."

"Who?" I nudged my bowl to the side with a frown.

Jeremy's eyes followed my bowl, obviously sizing it up for any leftovers he could scavenge. When it became clear that I'd practically licked the bowl clean, he lost interest.

"Prescott Pemberton. That artist guy that lived up on the bluff?"

Jeremy hooked a thumb over his shoulder as though that explained everything.

"Artist?" he asked. "He just came back to town a year ago?"

"Oh. *Oh.* I thought he went back to New York years ago or something?"

"He *was in* New York for years. He came back a year ago. Been here ever since," Jeremy explained.

He shot me a look as Shirley approached with our orders. We made small talk with her as she set my platter containing my giant pork tenderloin and heap of fries in front of me, then settled the giant bowl of chili in front of Jeremy. She pulled handfuls of crackers from her apron and scattered them on the table beside his bowl. After thanking her, Shirley disappeared behind the counter again.

I dipped my first French fry into the bowl of ranch on my platter and popped it into my mouth as Jeremy went about opening packages of crackers to crumble up in his chili. I picked at my fries, giving him time to prepare his bowl of chili to his liking and take his first bite before launching in with more questions.

"What happened?" I asked casually, lifting the top bun from my sandwich.

Pickles. Mustard. A few onions. Perfection. I laid the bun back atop the sandwich. Pork tenderloin poked out around the bun three inches in every direction. I was salivating.

"Well," Jeremy began as I lifted the sandwich to my mouth, "it's too early to tell, but the smell tells me poor guy was drunker than Mavis Attberry on the first of the month. Probably went for a walk, slipped, bashed his head…*dead.* Not sure if it was immediate or what yet. Not sure how long he was out there."

I cringed as I chewed.

"Nude, though?" I chuckled into my sandwich.

"Did I mention drunker than Mavis Attberry?"

"Even Mavis has the good sense to cover up."

"*Death by misadventure.*" Jeremy shrugged and shoveled chili into his mouth. "But the official call will be the Medical Examiner's. You get the newest Harrison Garner in yet?"

"A whole pile," I replied. "It's dwindling quickly. I'll put a copy aside for you. So…accident?"

Jeremy nodded slowly, chewing his food. "Looks like it right now. Spring in Head Rock Harbor, Jacks. There's always gotta be one fool doing something stupid to start off the season."

I shivered. "First time one of them ended up dead."

"First time for everything."

"You look like you haven't slept all night," I said. "When'd they find Prescott?"

Jeremy snorted.

"Not until dawn," he said, grinning over at me evilly. "But I was just going to bed."

I shook my head, unable to keep the smile from my face.

"You should have seen him," Jeremy leaned in conspiratorially. "I was over at Harper's last night—"

"As usual."

"—day laborer guy, maybe? Passing through, I guess." Jeremy ignored me. "Caught him staring at me from across the joint."

"As they usually do."

"Took him out back," Jeremy said with a mischievous shrug. "Then home. I'd just kicked him out so I could sleep before shift and the call came in. Didn't get a wink."

"Let's hope you didn't get anything else, either."

He frowned at me.

"They don't call you 'Germ' for nothing, man," I said.

Detective Jeremy "Germ" Morris grinned evilly as he slid his finger into my bowl of ranch. Chuckling and gagging, I swatted his hand away.

CHAPTER TWO

Head Rock Harbor is a small community nestled right off of highway 67 directly between the Quad Cities and Dubuque in East Central Iowa. The harbor isn't so much a harbor as it is a cove or inlet on the Mississippi River. Our community, as far back as I can remember, loves to make things sound much fancier than they deserve.

Regardless, Harbor Street, the oldest street in town, leads from highway 67, through town, right to the harbor. It's mainly a spot for the locals to take walks, picnic, and use as a slip to get their Jon boats out onto the river for some fishing or a pleasure cruise. The harbor itself is craggy and strewn with driftwood—in an aesthetically pleasing way—but the grassy area around the harbor and the slip makes a nice recreational area for families.

Naming a whole town after the feature, on the other hand, seems a stretch to me. However, when you're a speck on a state's map, and your population has never risen above five thousand, you do what you can to sound a little less backwoods. Not to say that Head Rock Harbor is...*backwoods*...it's simply a small community that would seem downright quaint to people from larger cities in the state. To someone from New York, we're practically unevolved.

However, being the middle place between two larger cities, we've become a point of interest for "city folk" looking to get away from the hustle and bustle. Exactly one hour from both Dubuque and the Quad Cities, Head Rock Harbor is seen as a quaint little town to visit on the weekends for city dwellers looking for a change of pace for a few days.

With a few bed and breakfast inns, a handful of antique shops, several cozy diners, a chocolatier, a bakery, the bookstore, a bar and grill, a tavern, some fine dining, and views of the river from everywhere in town, you could do worse for a weekend getaway. The city council has formed several subcommittees to keep tourism popular in town. There's always an event during the weekends, even in the dead of winter. Sure, the "Snowfall on the Square" yearly Christmas event can be a bit cheesy—especially when the weather refuses to participate—but it gives the townies and tourists something to do.

After lunch at Munchies, I somehow kept myself from stopping at Pain and Charlene's Chocolates. Instead, I went right back to the bookstore and parked myself behind the check-out counter. Within minutes, the store had a handful of shoppers, all of them whispering about Prescott Pemberton's misadventure in the harbor. While I felt bad for the guy—he was simply enjoying a harmless, drunken, nude stroll by the river, after all—a sly smile quirked at the corner of my lips.

I'd told Jeremy that the shop would be abuzz with the name of the victim after lunch.

Vindication!

Somehow, I wasn't so impressed and distracted with my own prediction coming true that I forgot to set aside a copy of Harrison Garner's latest book for Jeremy. The *New York Times* bestselling, riveting, action-packed book series about a smalltown Iowa cop had captivated our little town for the last five years. In the month following a new release of one of his books, Harrison Garner sales alone could keep the bookstore afloat. Not only did nearly every adult in town buy a copy, but the tourists would clean out a stack of the books in a single weekend. When I got my hands on signed copies, the rush of townies buying copies was chaotic.

God bless the authors who give bookstore owners hope. May they strive to yield their power benevolently and altruistically.

Not that I had to worry about selling books in the way that Charlene had to worry about chocolates, or Lardell and Shirley had to hustle to sell tenderloins. Head Rock Harbor Books was not a rental. I owned the building. As long as I paid the taxes each year, I'd never lose my home. Passed down to me by my aunt—my mom's sister—upon her death, Head Rock Harbor Books was the one store on Harbor Street that was guaranteed to survive. In some form or another, anyway.

By the end of the work day—Head Rock Harbor Books closes at seven o'clock on weeknights—Jeremy still hadn't stopped by to get his book. Having been up all night and then spending all day in the harbor investigating Prescott Pemberton's death, he had probably gone home after lunch and fallen asleep. I couldn't blame the guy for forgetting to stop by the shop.

As I went about my end of day routine, feeding Rattlesnatches, picking up any customer messes, a little light dusting, and cashing out the register, I slipped the book into a bag. At the front door, I switched off the main lights and gave Rattlesnatches a scratch behind the ears before exiting the store and locking the door behind me.

If you pick a spot anywhere in Head Rock Harbor it will never be further than a fifteen-minute walk from any other spot in town if you take your time. That's why I set off on foot in search of my dinner. It's not that I didn't have a car, but it was superfluous for getting around town. Besides, nearly three nights a week, I had dinner at Harper's Bar & Grill.

From the front door of the shop to the front door of Harper's is a ten-minute walk. However, for gay men, such as myself, it can be done in six. At half past seven, I was strolling up the wood plank path towards the bright signs of Harper's. The neon sign above the front door had seen better days, though it still glowed a vibrant pink that proclaimed "*Harper's Bar & G ill.*" One missing "r" didn't ruin anything, I supposed. The matching sign in the window of the front door proclaimed that the establishment was open for the evening.

The full name of the establishment is technically "Harper's Bar, Grill, Bait & Tackle," because there's a bar, a grill, and they sell bait and tackle in the back. However, after so many arguments with the health department, the name over the door got shortened. They continued to sell bait and tackle in the back, though. Possibly among other stuff that those of us in the know don't mention to people who wear badges for a living.

I pushed through the front door, glad to leave the crisp night air behind. The dining room to the left of the front door was still half-full from dinner service. The bar area, which held a few pool tables and a small dance floor, to the right of the front door, had caught the customers who had already eaten and were ready to top off their night.

The hostess stand next to the front door was unattended. It was typical, really. Heidi was a lovely girl but a horrible hostess. A quick glance around the joint and I locked eyes with her over at the bar. Heidi had her arm around Sawyer Robison's neck as he sipped a long neck and grinned like a puppy dog at her. The boy was barely old enough to drink. Having a woman like Heidi hanging off of him probably made his whole week. She gave me a wave and a smile.

"Seat yourself, Jackson!" she hollered. *"I'll let her know you're here."*

I gave her a nod and returned the smile. Hopefully, the bandages on Sawyer's neck from the incident with Rattlesnatches earlier in the day didn't dissuade Heidi from making his night. I sauntered over to an empty corner booth and slid into it. I pushed my jacket off and let it fall into the booth next to me, then I set the bag with Jeremy's book on top of it. I hadn't even had a chance to pick up a menu—not that I didn't have the thing memorized—before a shadow darkened my booth.

"Well, well, well. I guess you haven't forgotten us. His Royal Highness finally shows his face."

I didn't even bother to look up at the person standing beside my table. Instead, I grabbed the menu from the plastic holder at the other end of the table and began to flip through it.

"Hi, Deb."

"*Hi, Deb*," she parroted. "*Hi, Deb.* You know, my other children call me 'mom.'"

With a sigh, I tore my eyes from the menu and looked up at Deb Harper—owner of Harper's Bar & Grill. She also happened to be my mother. Her blue jeans were dark and crisp and her flannel shirt looked brand new. Apparently, she'd found some time to go shopping since I'd last seen her. We shared the same color of brown hair, but she had a lot more of it, and it was piled atop her head in a tangle of tied up loose curls. Fortunately, we did not share an affinity for the same shade of lipstick, because hers was bright red enough to be seen across town.

"Your other children?" I asked. "You adopt someone I don't know about? Do I have a brother and-or sister I have to worry about sharing my inheritance with?"

"Such as it is," she said with a grin. "I ain't knocked up if that's what you're asking. Not that I haven't been trying."

"This is why I call you 'Deb,'" I said. "Moms don't talk like that to their kids."

"Where you been?"

"Over at the store," I said. "I want the Philly cheesesteak and rings, please."

"Mmm," she mumbled, not bothering to jot anything down. "I know where you've been. I want to know why you haven't been here."

"I was here three days ago. I had the—"

"Philly cheesesteak and rings." Deb cut me off. "You're getting vegetables on the side tonight. No rings."

"Rings are onions. That's a vegetable."

"No rings."

"The cheesesteak has peppers in it. Another vegetable," I added.

"You're getting the cheesesteak and a salad." Deb jabbed me in the flesh of my upper arm with the pen she should have been using to write my ticket. "I won't hear anything else about it."

"This is why I haven't been here in three days," I said. "I don't need the abuse."

"So uppity and snippy," she said with a chuckle. "How's my boy?"

"Eh," I said with a shrug. "Things are good. How's tricks?"

"Now who's got a smart mouth?"

I smiled up at her.

"Cheesesteak and a side salad with ranch, Beau!" she hollered across the dining room.

Over at the passthrough to the kitchen, an arm shot out, a thumbs up at the end, before disappearing as quickly.

"Things are good," she said, sliding into the booth across from me. "Had to serve evictions on two of the trailers day before yesterday. So, we'll have some vacancies."

Deborah "Deb" Parker was the owner of Harper's Bar & Grill, and she also had the problematic distinction of being the owner and operator of Harper's Trailer Park. In the land behind the restaurant, a community of twenty-three trailers housed the less affluent citizens of Head Rock Harbor. It wasn't the lower economic class that made Harper's Trailer Park a problem for the town. It was the fact that several of the park's tenants were the biggest troublemakers in town. Mavis Attberry was the park's most notorious citizen.

"Please tell me one of them wasn't Mavis."

Deb snorted. "Even I'm not crazy enough to try and evict her. But, nah. She's paid up. That drinking doesn't keep her from making sure she keeps a roof over her head."

"Good," I said with a relieved sigh. "We don't need her and her shotgun roaming around town looking for places to sleep it off each night."

"She doesn't have it anymore."

"Huh?"

"The shotgun," Deb said. "It was taken—"

"By Marv." I finished her thought. "Yeah. I heard."

"You'd have heard sooner if you came around more often."

"Well, Shirley filled me in today."

"You hear about ole boy down there in the harbor?" Deb asked, leaning across the table.

I nodded. "Prescott Pemberton."

"If I'd known how drunk he actually was," Deb said, shaking her head. "Never would have let him leave."

"He was here last night?"

"He seemed dead sober when he left here," Deb said. "I told Germ that when he came 'round asking questions. Said the same thing to Marv when he followed up. *Go check with Bernie*, I told 'em. If he was walking around drunk last night, it wasn't from being here. He probably wandered over to Bernie's and tied one on with the rest of them idiots. We don't tolerate those drunken types of shenanigans over here at Harper's."

I couldn't help it. I shot a glance towards the bar.

"Nobody over there is doing anything wrong," Deb said, poking at me with the pen from across the table.

"I didn't say a word," I said, slapping her hand away.

"You were thinking something."

"I'm always thinking something. That's how brains work."

"You just think you're so smart."

The bell in the passthrough dinged, and Deb slid out of her booth without another word. Seconds later, she was sliding my plate in front of me. Philly cheesesteak with a side salad drenched in ranch dressing. I wondered if the rings wouldn't have been healthier.

"Thanks," I said.

"I'll put it on your tab."

We both grinned. I didn't have a tab at Harper's. Mom never let me pay for anything.

"You got the new Harrison Garner?" she asked. "Charlene said something about it coming out soon."

"Charlene came in here?" I scoffed as I unrolled my silverware. "What's she doing slumming around Harper's?"

"She's on her damn kick about the association. She wants to get every business in town involved now. So, she had to make the rounds and talk to the lower classes."

I laughed before stabbing at the salad with my fork.

"Yeah," I said. "I'll set a copy aside for you. In fact, I have one here. I was going to drop it by Jeremy's on my way home, but—"

"Oh," she cut me off, "he's over at the bar. You can give it to him before you leave."

Frowning, I tore my attention from my food to look over at the bar. Sure enough, Jeremy was stationed at the pool table in the dark back corner of the bar. Another man was lining up a shot and Jeremy was eyeing his backside lasciviously. I shook my head. Even with little to no sleep, the guy couldn't miss a night of prowling for tail. It didn't even matter if the tail might prove to not swing the way he needed. He still enjoyed the hunt.

"All right," I said. "I'll set another copy aside for you when I get back to the store."

"I'll swing by tomorrow for it," she said. "Now, eat all your food and I'll bring you some pie after."

As Deb walked away to tend to other tables, I hollered:

"You could have just let me have the rings!"

She cackled but didn't even bother looking back at me.

I tucked into my plate and scarfed my dinner down, ravenous from not having eaten since lunch time. I'm not the type of person who can go for hours without food, so I felt feral as I ate my dinner. By the time I was finished, most of the dining room had emptied and the diners had either bled into the bar or had made their way out of the restaurant to go home.

Deb made good on her promise and a giant slab of warm pecan pie with a scoop of vanilla ice cream on top was placed in front of me after dinner. I didn't devour it like I did my dinner, but instead savored every bite until I felt like I was going to explode when the plate was empty.

With a promise from me to come by more often, Deb cleared my plates away and I slipped my jacket back on. The bar of the restaurant was packed and the crowd was getting a bit too raucous for my liking, so I held onto Jeremy's bag as I exited the restaurant. Stuffing the bag in his mailbox would be a lot easier than trying to push through the sweaty bodies in the bar.

A few minutes later, I was standing on the street outside Jeremy's ranch-style house. When I opened his mailbox to deposit his book, I found the mailbox overflowing with mail. Grumbling, I extracted the wad of mail from the box and stuffed all of it into the bag with his book. I walked up the sidewalk to his house and set the bag on his front porch right in front of the door. Hopefully, he'd be unable to miss it.

I had a key to Jeremy's house, but something about entering someone's house without asking first—or without a really good reason—bothered me. Since Jeremy hadn't expected me to come by and let myself into his house, it didn't feel right to do so. He'd have to pick up the bag from the porch when he got home.

In case he came home from the bar a little worse for the wear, I pulled my phone out and shot off a quick text to let him know where to find his mail and the book. I didn't wait to see if he answered me. If I knew Jeremy, he was already going in for the kill with some unsuspecting man who had gotten more than he had bargained for when he agreed to play pool. I slipped my phone back in my pocket and speed walked back to the shop.

It was nearly nine o'clock when I was letting myself in the shop and locking up behind myself. I didn't bother turning on the shop lights. I wandered through the darkness to the stairs and made my way up to my apartment. Rattlesnatches was in his chair and he meowed a greeting at me as I approached. When I entered my apartment, he leapt from the chair, a soft "thump" indicating his movements.

Together, we went inside the small apartment and shut the door behind us. It was a habit of mine to close and lock my apartment door when I retired for the night. Even though the entire shop was basically my home, having a locked door to the apartment always made me feel safer when I slept. Even if someone broke into the shop, at least I'd be locked inside my apartment. Not that anyone couldn't also break into my apartment once they were inside the shop, but at least maybe I'd hear the ruckus downstairs and the locked apartment door would give me time to arm myself and call the police before they got to me.

Of course, I never told anyone about this habit of mine. In a town like Head Rock Harbor, burglaries and murders are nonexistent. Anyone scared enough to lock every door in their house at night was crazier than the nonexistent criminals.

I checked Rattlesnatches' water bowl and topped it off. I dumped a handful of food into his other bowl as a treat—in case he got hungry in the middle of the night. Then I changed into my pajamas and slipped under the covers of my bed. I flicked on the lamp and grabbed the novel I was halfway through from my bedside table. By the time Rattlesnatches found a spot he was comfortable in next to my head, I was lost in my book.

CHAPTER THREE

"I don't know what got into my noggin, Jackson!" Lila Westbrook was shaking her head as she folded the blindingly white towels on the check-out counter. "Harrison Garner's new book was the whole reason I came over yesterday!"

On Tuesdays and Wednesdays, Head Rock Harbor Books is only open until lunch time. I close the shop completely on Sundays. However, Sundays are for relaxation and avoiding all social situations if possible, so Tuesday and Wednesday afternoons are used for deliveries and networking.

Mrs. Lila Westbrook, the owner of the Head Rock Harbor Inn, had been in the store the day before—Monday—when Rattlesnatches had launched his attack on my clientele right before lunch. The chaos had rattled everyone's nerves, so Mrs. Westbrook had left the store with a few paperbacks, but had forgotten to grab a copy of Harrison Garner's latest book.

When she had called over to the shop on Tuesday morning, I had been more than happy to offer to deliver it to her after I closed the shop at lunch.

"Well, I know what landed on it," I said. "My cat."

Mrs. Westbrook chuckled. "Well, my brain was rattled even before that. It was a day, wasn't it?"

She gave me a look over the top of her spectacles but her hands didn't stop folding towels. Mrs. Westbrook was a gossip—like most everyone else in town—but she never slouched when it came to running her inn.

"I suppose," I said, laying the bag containing the book on the counter.

The plastic bag was emblazoned with the name of Head Rock Harbor Books in a deep shade of maroon that matched the woodwork on the shop's exterior and interior.

"What with the body…," she prompted me.

I nodded slowly. I love gossip. However, it's never clear with whom and when it is okay to gossip. Not that I knew much more about Prescott Pemberton's death than anyone else in town, but I didn't want to let information slip to someone who may not have heard it already. There were two reasons for this.

One, everyone would assume that Jeremy had leaked information to me about his investigation. While it was often true, I didn't want people assuming it. I didn't want my best friend to get in trouble with his job or lose any respectability he had managed to garner. Two, once the hornet's nest has been kicked, then starts settling down, you don't want to be the guy who gives it another nudge. Head Rock Harbor rarely had any news worth sharing, so when something scandalous actually happened, it was difficult for the townsfolk to let it go for a long time.

I didn't want to be talking about Prescott Pemberton through spring and into summer.

"I haven't heard much," I said.

Disappointed, Mrs. Westbrook's shoulders slumped, but her hands kept folding.

"Do you need help?" I asked, pointing at the stack of freshly washed hotel towels.

"No, no, no." She waved me off with a friendly hand. "Don't you dare. You were nice enough to deliver my book. How much do I owe you, by the way?"

"Twenty-five," I said. "Tax included. I sure don't mind helping."

Another slap to my hand as I reached for the pile of towels forced me to give up on being polite. With a chuckle, I held my hands up defensively as Mrs. Westbrook reached into her pocket. Pulling a few bills out, she sorted them thoughtfully before handing me a five and a twenty.

"Thanks," I said.

"I just love his books," Mrs. Westbrook said, sliding the bag off the counter to stow it underneath. "As soon as I get into bed tonight, I'll start reading."

"Harrison Garner definitely has a fan base in Head Rock Harbor." I agreed. "And everywhere else."

"You should get him to do a signing at the store!" she exclaimed as though she was the first person to have the thought. "Can you imagine what that would do for tourism?"

"Well—"

"Harrison Garner in your shop would have the whole town down there. The books would fly off the shelves! Not to mention all the tourists who'd drive in from the Quad Cities and Dubuque! You really should see if you can get him, Jackson. And Ms. Charlene Hardy would hug you 'round your neck 'til you passed out."

With a laugh, I pulled out my wallet and deposited Mrs. Westbrook's bills.

"I've talked to his agent. You'd have better luck getting J.D. Salinger to make an appearance," I said. "Even now that he's dead. Besides, I've heard that this might be his last mystery novel."

"*What? No!*"

"I guess coming up with new mysteries is more difficult than us readers would believe," I said with a shrug.

"I'd just *hate* that!" Mrs. Westbrook slapped the counter gently. "I come to look forward to each new book he releases."

"You and everyone else." I chuckled. "I guarantee that even if he keeps writing, he won't come to some little shop like mine to sign books. But I can't get mad since sales of his books make me a decent amount of money."

Mrs. Westbrook huffed out a disappointed puff of air and stomped her foot. It was adorable.

"He doesn't seem to enjoy fame, I guess," I said.

"Well," she sighed, then brightened, "I suppose you did your best."

"I did."

"If he ever has a change of heart, though…,"

"You'll be the first to know after me," I assured her.

Brightening further, she went back to folding her towels.

"Well, we have to do something about the tourism around here. It's fine, I suppose," she prattled on, "but things could be better."

I couldn't disagree with her, so I kept my mouth shut.

"Two or three rooms rented a week isn't going to have me retiring early, I'll tell you that much. The big city folks from back east come swooping in to stay for a week to try out *small town life* isn't doing much, either. Not that I mind the money, of course."

"Of course." I chuckled.

The pile of straw-colored cotton candy on Mrs. Westbrook's headed wobbled as she carried on animatedly. Her copious decolletage carried on the dance a few seconds longer. Never much one for the female form—or boobs in general—I still found myself staring for a moment too long. Mrs. Westbrook could have been crowned the Dolly Parton of East Central Iowa and I wouldn't have been shocked, though she was still a few decades younger than Dolly.

"They use more towels than anyone I've seen in my life," she said, holding up and shaking an unfolded towel at me for emphasis. "How one person can go through so many is beyond me. You won't find us Iowans being so wasteful. It's always the ones from back east. I swear—*between me and you*—there are more towels here than we had to begin with!"

I laughed and shrugged at the inconvenience put upon the owner of our best inn.

"I guess we should be glad we can attract tourists from that far away?"

Mrs. Westbrook's mouth turned up, and for a moment, I thought I was going to get an earful for disagreeing with her. Barely five feet tall and slight enough to be blown over by a stiff breeze, Mrs. Westbrook could still produce an intimidating scowl. However, her expression quickly changed.

"It's the river life," she carried on. "We have the river, a decent nightlife for those lookin' to *slum it* with the *normal folks*, good Midwestern food that sticks to your ribs, great shops, and big enough cities nearby that they don't feel too far from home."

"That we do."

"Well, you're probably right," she said. "I guess it's best to be thankful for what you've got."

"Glad you see that I'm right," I said, teasing her.

Mrs. Westbrook clicked her tongue at me playfully before tossing the unfolded towel in my face. Laughing, I yanked it away and politely handed it back to her. Somehow, I managed to keep my nose from turning up. She may have been able to get her towels blindingly white, but the smell that wafted up my nose after having one stuffed in my face was unpleasant. Something slightly fishy burned at my nose hairs.

Since Mrs. Westbrook didn't seem to notice the smell—and I couldn't smell the towels from where they sat on the counter—I shook the thought away.

"I'll tell you what, though," Mrs. Westbrook leaned in, "playing full time housekeeper to one guest isn't worth the money. The city folks have more demands and make more messes than folks from around these parts."

"I'm sure," I said, patting her hand. "Well, if you do end up needing help, I'm free all evening and tomorrow afternoon and evening."

"You're just a dear," Mrs. Westbrook said. "I'll be fine. I've been doing this for twenty years. But if you see my husband and his fishing pole down at the harbor, tell him to bring home dinner tonight. That's *not* a request."

With the promise to tell her husband to bring home dinner if I saw him, I said goodbye to Mrs. Westbrook and exited the Head Rock Harbor Inn.

I strolled the few blocks back over to Harbor Street and hooked a right at the corner of Munchies Café. My plan had been to head back home and whip something up in my small kitchenette for lunch now that my deliveries were done. However, as soon as I rounded the corner onto Harbor Street, my eyes landed on Charlene Hardy. She was huffing and marching down the sidewalk, distracted by the piles of fliers cradled in her arms.

The redness of her cheeks and her aggressive gait let me know that she was in a mood. Not wanting to have a heated discussion with her about the HSBOA, I made an executive decision and slipped into Munchies.

Instead of taking my usual seat at the booth in the front window, I slithered to the back of the dining room and sat down at a two-seater in the corner. Within seconds, Shirley was standing tableside staring down at me.

"Two days in a row?" she asked. "To what do we owe this honor?"

"It just seemed easier than making something at home," I mumbled, letting my jacket fall off my shoulders onto my chair back.

I glanced over at the front window of Munchies in time to catch Charlene stomping by, muttering angrily to herself. Shirley, catching onto my glance, turned her head to see what I'd found such a special interest in outside. Chuckling she turned back to me.

"Avoiding Charlene, are you?"

I waved her off. "I'm just not in the mood today."

"No judgment from me." Shirley grinned. "I had to run her off earlier. She can't take a hint. No one around here wants anything to do with that association."

Nodding, I began to speak, but Shirley stopped me.

"Yeah, yeah. Pork loin, fries, ranch to dip, cole slaw."

I smiled sheepishly.

"You know she's started going around to people's houses if they won't entertain her at their businesses?" Shirley asked. "Showed up at Bernie's house at the butt crack of dawn the other morning since he wouldn't talk to her at the bar the night before."

"Really?"

"Sure as we're talking to each other," Shirley said. "He was nicer than me. I would have fired off a warning shot. He just told her to get gone so he could go back to sleep."

The two of us chuckled and Shirley patted my shoulder.

"I'll have your food right up, hon."

"Thanks."

As Shirley headed to the passthrough to let Lardell know to whip up my usual, my phone buzzed in my pocket. I slipped it out far enough to read the text notification banner. It was from Jeremy.

In need of a homecooked meal. I'll be over around seven.

He hadn't even asked. He had stated. Like any true friend would do. Smiling, I unlocked my phone and replied with a simple "ok." Since I wasn't cooking for lunch, it wouldn't kill me to make a real dinner for once.

CHAPTER FOUR

The idea wasn't complicated, nor was the speech to present it to me long, but it didn't take a genius to know that the proposition Charlene was presenting was in bad taste. And that was being generous with labeling her idea.

"I just think it would be a nice thing if we helped out his family by doing it," she said. "Our community extending a helping hand in their hour of need, you know?"

Charlene had one leg inside of the shop, blocking me from closing the door. It was a position she'd taken up as soon as I'd shown up downstairs to see who was knocking. Everyone in town knows that the shop is closed Tuesday afternoons, so when I heard the pounding, I'd been dumb enough to investigate, thinking that there was possibly an emergency. Instead, I'd found Charlene Hardy, fliers in hand and an idea brewing in her skull.

"Don't you think it's a little soon?" I asked.

"Oh, goodness, no," she replied. "These things are awful for families anyway, aren't they? Anything to make final arrangements for a loved one easier is a blessing, isn't it?"

"His body was found yesterday, Charlene."

"I know, I know." She sighed empathetically. "I can't imagine what his family must be thinking, out there back east. I heard they'll be arriving in a few days. Or maybe they were going to have the body sent to them. I can't really remember what Chief Bucksworth said. But this will give them one last thing to worry about, won't it?"

Marv—Chief Bucksworth—had probably not said one word to Charlene Hardy about Prescott Pemberton. He was a notoriously taciturn man, especially when it came to the job. However, to justify the ideas that popped into her head, Charlene was more than willing to stretch the truth a bit. Marv had probably said "we'll see" when Charlene asked what was going to happen, and she had concocted an entire dramatic three act play in her head.

"Calling the family and offering to have an auction for his art and belongings might be in bad taste right now, Charlene," I said, pushing the door a bit towards her.

I hoped she'd get the hint, but Charlene proved to be as unmovable as she always was when an idea was stuck in her head.

"Well," she continued, ignoring me, "I'm more than happy to do the dirty work and talk to the family, of course. But the community really responds to you, Jackson. And you know all about art and antiques and what things are worth. All that reading you do! You're probably the most educated Head Rock Harbor citizen! If the family agrees, you could go up to his house with me and see if there's anything worth having an auction for, then help me assure the community it's all in good taste and there are things worth bidding on."

Sighing, I let go of the door and crossed my arms over my chest casually. A quick glance at the wall clock over the check-out counter told me that Jeremy would be over for dinner in less than twenty minutes. Thankfully, I had almost everything prepared and in the oven. I simply had to get rid of Charlene before the smell of smoke started drifting down the stairs and into the shop.

"With what end in mind?" I asked the obvious question. "If the family actually doesn't take offense to a stranger calling up and asking to sell off his stuff, the money would go to them. It won't benefit the HSBOA or Head Rock Harbor. And it might just make us look like crackpots to the family, they'll start the whispers, and—"

"Tourism!" Charlene announced as if I was dense. "Prescott Pemberton's artwork and personal belongings up for auction? We'd get folks from Dubuque, Des Moines, the Quad Cities, even Chicago up here for that, Jackson."

"I don't think Prescott is that famous."

"A dead artist?" Charlene snorted. "We all know what happens to the value of an artist's work after they die, Jackson."

"Wow."

Charlene collected herself, obviously realizing that she had said the quiet part out loud. Straightening the front of her shirt casually, she brushed away an invisible piece of fluff, screwed up her thin lips in a tight smile and soldiered on.

"His family won't have to pay to have all of his things shipped out east. They won't have to come out here to deal with the mess. It's a service the community can provide to help his family during a very trying time," Charlene explained. "*And* it will be a fun event for the community."

"Picking over a dead artist's life work. Fun." I let my arms fall to my sides.

"Jackson, I—"

"Look," I said, reaching up to grab the door again, "if Marv will get you in touch with the family, he thinks it's a good idea, and the family isn't against it, I'll come check out the house with you and let you know if it's even worth it. But I can't guarantee I'll know any better than any estate appraiser—which is who you should really be speaking to right now."

Charlene lit up at the beginning of my sentence and ignored the ending of it.

"Oh, wonderful!" she exclaimed. "Thank you, Jackson. Here. Now take one of these—"

She shoved two of her HSBOA fliers in my free hand and I was too slow to stop her.

"—and we'll talk soon. Maybe tomorrow!"

Charlene Hardy disappeared from the front entrance of Head Rock Harbor Books as quickly as she'd appeared. Shaking my head, I eased the door closed and relocked it.

Rattlesnatches was at my feet, staring up me. He shook his head as if to say: *I hear ya', brother.*

"She's insane," I said.

Rattlesnatches blinked. I was going to assume one blink was "yes" and two was "no."

"Come on."

The two of us turned and walked back to the stairs and made our way back up to the apartment. I stopped only briefly at the check-out counter to straighten the propped-up display copy of Harrison Garner's new book. Smart shop owners give bestselling items extra love and care if they have any idea what they're doing with their business.

Back upstairs, I cracked the oven for a quick peek and found everything was on schedule. The dish I'd decided to make for dinner was browning up nicely, so I slid into one of the chairs at my small kitchen table where the book I was in the middle of reading was waiting.

A few minutes later and the timer was chiming. It was no surprise that I had reached a climactic scene in my novel, but finding out what happened next wasn't as important as not burning dinner. If I hadn't been expecting company, a little char on the casserole might not have been a big deal, but since I wasn't dining alone, I decided attending to the food was more important. So, I used the fly leaf of the book to mark my place and set my book aside with a sigh. Rattlesnatches looked over from his perch on my bed and blinked lazily.

He understood my struggle.

I had barely pulled the casserole dish out of the oven when I heard the front door of the shop open. Typically, someone getting into a locked shop-slash-house was a thing of concern, but I'd given Jeremy a key to the place years ago. It was always good to have someone who could check in on Rattlesnatches when I was away or check things out for me if something odd happened. The fact that the person I chose was my best friend *and* a police officer made the situation perfect.

Jeremy's footsteps sounded on the stairs as I was transferring a trivet and the dish to the small two-seater table in the kitchenette.

"*Honey!*" he hollered. "*I'm home!*"

"I'm in the kitchen, darling!" I hollered back with a chuckle.

Fortunately, I had managed to set the casserole dish on the trivet before Jeremy swooped into the apartment and wrapped his arms around me. Before I could stop him, he had dipped me, as if performing a ballroom dance, then began to lift me, his lips puckered. Covering his face with my hand and shoving him away, I wiggled out of his arms.

"Don't be a weirdo," I said, wiping my hand on my leg to rid it of the spit from his lips.

"Is that any way to treat your husband after a long day of work?" he asked, pretending to be hurt.

He dropped into the chair at the table and immediately began to appraise the dish at the center of the table. I slipped into the chair across from him.

"Husband?" I chuckled. "The day someone calls you their husband I'll drop dead from shock."

"What's that supposed to mean?" Jeremy grinned at me. "I shut the lights off downstairs so we won't be disturbed."

A roll of my eyes was my response. Reminding my best friend that he was never going to be the settling down type seemed a waste of good words.

"Did you close the light switch box?" I asked.

"Of course," Jeremy looked offended. "I know better than to leave it up."

We both looked over at Rattlesnatches on my bed, then at each other, before laughing.

"Chicken cobbler," I said, reaching for the serving spoon.

"I see that," Jeremy looked at the dish and rubbed his hands together greedily. "My favorite."

"There're sodas and beers in the fridge," I cocked my head towards the fridge as I plunged the serving spoon into the casserole.

Jeremy rose from the table and took the two full steps required to cross the kitchenette to the fridge.

"You want a beer or a soda?" he asked.

"Soda, please."

Jeremy grabbed a can of Pabst Blue Ribbon for himself and a can of root beer for me. By the time he had slid back into his seat and put my can in front of my plate, I had served him up a heaping helping of the chicken cobbler.

"It looks great, Jacks," he said, reaching for his fork. "Thanks."

"I picked up a pecan pie from the store," I said. "I didn't want to hear you complain about not having dessert again."

"Silence!" Jeremy demanded playfully. "I am always a gracious guest and will not hear slander for a moment."

He deposited the forkful of food into his mouth, stared at me with wide eyes that languidly shut with pleasure before releasing a chorus of appreciative moans.

"Like I said…*weirdo*."

Jeremy laughed and chewed his mouthful of food. "It's really good, Jacks."

"Always is. I've made it for you enough I could do it with my hands tied."

"One day I'll have to marry you," Jeremy sighed and shoved another heaping bit into his mouth. "Just so I can have this whenever I want."

"Why buy the cow when you can get the milk for free?" I shrugged as I dug into my food.

"Fair." Jeremy looked thoughtful. "But someone ought to make an honest man out of you one day."

"I'm the one who needs to be reined in?"

Jeremy chuckled and continued to eat.

"Speaking of *honest men*," I began as I chewed, "you out on the prowl again tonight? Or are you working?"

Jeremy chewed and looked lost in thought for a moment.

"I'm off tonight," he said. "And two nights of prowling might be enough before a break is needed. Gotta recharge before going hunting again, right?"

"I wouldn't know."

"That's an understatement," Jeremy guffawed. "When's the last time you had an unrelated man in this apartment?"

"I have an unrelated man in here now."

"You know what I mean."

"Last decade? I don't know." I smiled sheepishly.

"That's what I'm talking about, Jacks." Jeremy jabbed at me with his fork. "You have to get out there and get some action. You're going to end up like Belinda if you don't watch out."

Belinda, my aunt who had previously owned Head Rock Harbor Books and left it to me in her will, had died an infamous spinster. By her own choice. She'd had no use for romance or marriage. Books had been her one true love. Dying of a heart attack and being found the following morning lying amongst the stacks had been her dream come true.

"You get out there and get enough action for both of us."

"I do my best," Jeremy said. "Anyway. How's sales? Life?"

"Good, I suppose. Head Rock Harbor Books will be open next month, if that's what you're wondering. I saw Mom last night. Saw you as well, but you looked busy, so I didn't say 'hi.'"

"Huh?"

"I was at Harper's for dinner last night," I explained as we ate. "After I ate, I saw you on the prowl in the bar at the pool tables. I didn't want to bother you."

Jeremy chuckled. "Yeah. I had a little fun. But I was at home, in bed, at a decent hour."

"I'll choose to believe you."

He snorted. "Okay. Maybe I wasn't alone. Do you have my Harrison Garner book? You said you'd hold a copy for me."

"I left it on your porch in a bag along with the week worth of mail that was stuffed in your box."

"Oh," Jeremy shoved another forkful of food in his mouth, "I must have missed it. I'll get it later when I go home. Thanks."

"No need to thank me," I said. "Just give me twenty-five dollars."

Laughing, Jeremy and I finished our plates and both agreed on seconds. When it comes to chicken cobbler—Jeremy's favorite dish that I make for him—we both can't get enough. Half of a large casserole dish is consumed in one meal.

After dinner, I covered the casserole and stored it in the fridge before bringing out the boxed pie from the store. Jeremy and I polished off a large slice apiece before giving up. Together, we washed dishes—me on the scrubbing, him on the drying. When we were done, we found ourselves back at the table, holding our bellies and groaning.

"Charlene Hardy came by right before you showed up tonight," I said. "Have you talked to her?"

"I've talked to everybody, Jacks. Everyone has an opinion about Prescott Pemberton and why he was walking around nude in the middle of the night in the harbor," Jeremy chuckled uncomfortably.

"She wants to call his family and offer to auction off all of his belongings to 'help them out,'" I began. "She actually thinks Marv will hook her up with the family to ask them."

He shook his head. "That woman isn't living if she isn't putting her nose in somewhere it doesn't belong. She's worse than Mavis. Well, maybe. At least Charlene isn't seeing ghosts."

"Ghosts?" I frowned.

"Drunk old bird's theory for Prescott Pemberton's death is he was being haunted. Said she was walking home from the bar—*crawling is more like it if you ask me*—and saw him out in the harbor with a ghost. Must have been within minutes of his death. Mavis thinks the ghosts got him."

I rolled my eyes. "Forty years of five-dollar bottles of whisky will do that to a gal, I suppose."

"I just took her home and told her to sleep it off. Granted, she was telling me this right after lunch, so take that as you will."

"As an officer of the law," I teased, "you have to follow up on all leads, though. Right? If Mavis says she saw ghosts killing Prescott, you have to investigate."

Jeremy rolled his eyes.

"Detective Morris," I said, "as a tax-paying citizen of Head Rock Harbor, I demand—"

"Let it go, Jacks," he groaned, his head rolling back on his shoulders. "Don't you start acting like every other crazy in this town. The guy fell and hit his head."

"Calm down." I laughed. "I'm just teasing you."

Jeremy pushed his long legs out to stretch and the holster at his thin waist shifted slightly. If it weren't for the belt, there'd be nothing to hold Jeremy's pants up.

"Sounds right for Mavis, though," I said. "Well, you aren't working tonight. You're off tomorrow. And you don't plan on going out prowling and looking for ghosts…"

"Yeah?" Jeremy asked.

"How about a movie?"

"As long as I get to choose," he said as a grin bloomed on his face.

"Deal."

CHAPTER FIVE

DEATH BY MISADVENTURE. *Local Artist Found Dead in Harbor.*

The Head Rock Harbor Herald had the decency to leave Prescott Pemberton's state of un-dress out of the headline. Of course, it would have been a much more eye-catching headline if they had mentioned he was naked as a jay bird, but who was I to tell someone how to write? I stood in the doorway of the store, holding the door open with my hip as I scanned the front page of the paper.

Not much ever happens in Head Rock Harbor, and considering its size, our daily paper is only a few pages. A couple of headlines covering the most important news in town, some coupons for groceries and local stores and eateries, an entertainment section, a few op-eds, and a comics section. One can read the entire newspaper in under thirty minutes.

"Back inside," I casually nudged Rattlesnatches with the heel of my slipper when his little head peeked out the door. "I didn't save you from the streets to have you get run over."

A small "mew" escaped Rattlesnatches' mouth but he obeyed. Once he had slunk back inside, I looked up and down the street in the early morning light, yawning and scratching my head. I was still in my pajamas and my robe was belted tightly around my waist. I still had an hour to eat breakfast and shower before I opened the shop until lunchtime.

So far, on Harbor Street, there wasn't much early morning traffic. I could smell the aroma from the ovens down at Pain, and I could hear work-related noise drifting over from Charlene's next door, but otherwise, the street was still quiet and empty. The typical "hustle and bustle" of small-town living in Head Rock Harbor.

My preparation for the morning and the morning itself were uneventful. Since the shop is only open during the morning hours on Wednesdays, it was only my hardcore readers who showed up to shop. Though Head Rock Harbor is a fairly progressive town, and has much more to offer than a town its size has the right to, we don't have a library. Though I'm not entirely happy about the fact, it does benefit Head Rock Harbor Books' bottom line. It also ensures that I never go a day without at least a handful of sales.

My cozy mystery, romance, and young adult readers kept the morning lively. It always amazed me how many books a romance reader could go through in a week, though no judgement is doled out on my part. Reading or picking up a book—no matter the book—is perfectly acceptable at all times. Readers and book people are the best people.

That's not me simply thinking about my bank account, either.

When lunchtime was creeping near, the shop was empty and Rattlesnatches had curled up in his bed at the front window. A beam of warm sunlight was keeping him snug as a bug. With only fifteen minutes left in the morning hours, I decided to close up shop early. Going through my closing routine that I've completed a million times, I was ready to head out for lunch within seven minutes—one of my personal best times.

Rattlesnatches hadn't moved from his spot, so I lifted the light switch cover, flipped off the lights, and slipped out unnoticed. After locking up, I glanced through the front window and confirmed that my leaving the store had absolutely no effect on Rattlesnatches' nap. Nothing kept him from chasing his dreams. Literally.

"Jackson Harper, you have been avoiding me!"

Freezing in place at the sound of the voice behind me, I was left in limbo between looking through the front window of the shop and turning to walk away for lunch. Linda Wagner's voice could turn anybody to stone. It suddenly occurred to me that if I had waited those last fifteen minutes before closing up for the day, I might have avoided the oncoming assault. Of course, Head Rock Harbor's Honorable Mayor Linda Wagner might very well may have been waiting until noon for me to step outside.

Linda Wagner, the mayor of Head Rock Harbor for—*somehow*—six consecutive terms never confronted business owners in their actual businesses. She saw it as distasteful since having a *serious discussion* with the mayor in front of customers might scare them off and cost the owners sales. When you're a politician looking to keep some amity with business owners who also happen to vote, you don't do such things.

However, Linda Wagner felt that once a business owner's feet struck pavement, all was fair game.

"Linda," I said, turning in the direction from which her voice came, "how can I be avoiding you? I'm here seven days a week. All day. Every day."

"You weren't here yesterday afternoon!"

Linda was standing near the curb, her arm laced through her husband's. Mark Wagner—pink cheeked and smiling apologetically—had the handles of numerous shopping bags laced over his free arm. From the looks of things, I was the last stop in Linda Wagner's reign of terror on Harbor Street. Of course, since she had shopped at all of the other stores, I was apparently the only one she was looking to give a talking to about…whatever.

"Tuesdays and Wednesdays are both half days," I said.

Mark shifted awkwardly, his pleated khakis and lime green polo shirt looking stiff enough to be paper doll clothes. His Hush Puppies looked newly purchased and his graying hair looked as though it recently encountered shellac. Combined with the smile and pink cheeks, he was the personification of "uncomfortable." I couldn't blame him. I'd spent ten seconds with his wife and an itch was creeping up my neck.

"Well, that must be nice," Linda said, crossing her arms under her breast. "And then Sundays off as well."

Her pressed cerulean pantsuit, sensible shoes, and expertly coiffed hair looked anything but mayoral. In fact, between the color of her pantsuit and Mark's lime green polo, I felt as though I was speaking with a pair of highlighters.

"I don't know when you sacrifice your chickens to Jesus, but I do it on Sunday." I shrugged.

"What?" She gulped.

Mark coughed.

"What can I help you with, Linda?" I asked.

"You've been avoiding me," she said again. "You know what I'm talking about, Jackson."

I did know what she was talking about, but she didn't know for certain that I did.

"Remind me?" I asked, turning and walking down the street.

Forcing Linda and Mark to chase after me to talk was a way of trying to shake them. Of course, it didn't work. Linda was too tenacious for such tricks.

"Well," Linda broke free from Mark in a huff to rush up beside me, matching my speed, "I've been trying to get you to organize a Gay Pride parade for ages."

"This is the second year you've asked," I said. "I don't know if that qualifies as *ages*."

"You completely ignored me last year, and—"

"You mentioned it in the middle of May. Pride is in June," I explained, continuing to walk. "You didn't really give me much time, Linda."

"—well, that's beside the point." She waved a dismissive hand. "This year I've caught you in March. There's no reason you can't throw something together *this* year."

Frowning, I stopped in the middle of the sidewalk, forcing Linda to stop to face me. Mark nearly walked over himself in his attempt to avoid a collision with us. Linda had a little bit of the middle-age spread about her, but she wore it well. Mark, on the other hand, was showing his years a little worse. His face had turned from pink to red in the short walk we'd taken.

"*Throw something*—" I frowned at her. "A Pride event takes planning. And more than one person planning it."

Linda shrugged dramatically. "Recruit some of your friends. We need to get with the times, Jackson. A Pride parade this year—*at the minimum*—would bring in some tourism for a weekend. The HSBOA is struggling to get off the ground—as you know—and we might even get mentions in some of the bigger cities' papers. We might even get a spot on the news."

"Look," I said with a sigh, "I appreciate how progressive you, the HSBOA, and the rest of Head Rock Harbor attempt to be, Linda. But our town is just not big enough for a Pride parade. Maybe a Pride themed cookout in the park or something? But a parade seems like overkill."

"Well, can't you—"

"And, honestly, I don't feel like being knighted the Town Queer, either," I finished.

Linda, sputtering and laying a hand to her chest, made the corner of my mouth turn up devilishly. Mark coughed.

"I never—"

"I'm not a mascot, Linda," I said, and started walking again.

Linda and Mark caught up quickly.

"I'm not trying to make you into the…the…a mascot," Linda stammered. "However, you are a prominent business owner who *happens* to be gay. Who else would be better to organize a Pride event for Head Rock Harbor?"

"Ask Jeremy," I said. "Detective Morris."

She waved me off. Mark was barely keeping up with us. "He's busy."

"And I'm not?" I scoffed and walked faster.

"*Jackson Harper*," Linda stopped in the middle of the sidewalk and huffed, "*if you do not stop right this instant.*"

With a sigh, I stopped to face her. Mark let out a gulp of breath that told me how thankful he was for the sudden stop. I felt bad for the guy. Unless he was at Linda's service, he was of no use to her. It was obvious he would have much rather have been at home, in his recliner, remote in one hand and beer in the other. I couldn't say I blamed him. He was nearly sixty. Chasing his ambitious wife up and down Harbor Street should have been the last thing on his mind on a random Wednesday.

"What, Linda?" I asked.

"Pride event," she said, jabbing a finger into my chest, her nail threatening to dig through the material of my shirt. "Figure something out."

I nearly reminded Linda Wagner that she wasn't my real mother, but I figured she wouldn't see the humor in such a statement. Instead, I settled for how I responded to most of the pushy people in town. A vague promise to see what I could do.

"I'll brainstorm some ideas," I said. "That work for you?"

Linda's face lit up and her demeanor completely changed. No longer was I confronted by the steely-faced mayor on a mission, but instead I was given the pleasant and pleased grin of a woman whose mission had been accomplished. The mayor didn't have to be told that I hadn't actually promised her anything. She'd figure it out when June came and went without a Pride event.

"Wonderful," Linda said, suppressing her excitement. "Well, now that *that* is settled, I have many other items on my list today."

Without another word, she turned on her heels and marched off in the direction from which we had come. A glance down the street proved that she had parked her car on the street not far from the bookstore. She had been lying in wait for me to step outside after all. Mark gave me another apologetic smile before turning and chasing after his wife.

Shaking my head, I watched the woman who had presided as mayor over Head Rock Harbor since I was a small child clip-clop away in her kitten heels. Mark chased after Linda as though she was holding his inhaler and he was in serious need of a hit. Which, when I thought about it, could have been completely true.

"*We all do our part to make Head Rock Harbor the weekend destination in East-Central Iowa, Jackson!*" Linda shouted over her shoulder as the distance between us increased. "*Marv was looking for you!*"

I didn't respond. With a roll of my eyes, I turned and carried on in the direction I had been headed. Of course, Marv was looking for me. Charlene Hardy had probably gone straight from my bookstore to the police department after assaulting me the previous evening. Just as Linda Wagner was going to blame me for the lack of an annual Pride event in Head Rock Harbor, the Chief was going to blame me for Charlene Hardy's crass ideas.

A few minutes later, I was strolling up the walk to Jeremy's house. He hadn't had his wallet on him the night before during dinner to pay for his copy of the Harrison Garner novel, so I'd told him I'd stop by after work the following day. It was the following day and it was after work. I am a man of my word and protector of my bank account.

At Jeremy's front door, I grumbled with frustration to find the bag containing his copy of the book and all of his mail was still sitting on the porch. Fortunately, though the weather been cool, it had been sunny. When I lifted the bag, everything inside was dry and in perfect condition. I'd barely raised my fist to knock on the aluminum frame of the front screen when Jeremy's voice stopped me.

"You got here earlier than I expected," he hollered.

I glanced over my shoulder to find him jogging up the sidewalk behind me.

"Oh," I said, turning to meet him. "I thought you were off today. I figured you'd just be getting out of bed right about now."

Jeremy chuckled as he bounded up onto the porch to stand in front of me. His hair was tussled just so and his clothes were wrinkled enough that I didn't need to ask where he had been.

"I thought I'd get here before you," he said. "Did you close up early?"

"Fifteen minutes," I said, handing him the bag. "But Linda and Mark caught me, and—"

"Pride event?" he asked with a sheepish grin.

"Mm." I cocked an eyebrow.

"Sorry, Jacks," he said. "You're the Designated Gay. You know that."

I turned my nose up at him. Not simply because he had said nearly the exact same thing I'd said to Linda Wagner, but because of the smell. A vague fishy smell was wafting off of my best friend. Although I find it easier to ask rude questions if someone is your friend, I tend to not mention body odor to anyone unless they need to be told to wash up before going out.

"You here to take a shower?" I asked.

"Among other things."

"Okay." I didn't need to mention the smell. If he had been rolling around in the shallow end of the river with the previous night's conquest, that was no longer my business. "Give me twenty-five bucks and I'll be on my way."

"Oh! Right!" Jeremy reached into his back pocket and extracted his wallet.

Moments later, I was sliding the money from his hand and into my pocket.

"I thought you didn't have your wallet last night?"

"I didn't."

"Well, if you went out *hunting* when you left my place after the movie, then—"

"I came home first."

"Then why was the bag still sitting on the porch?" I asked.

"You ask a lot of questions, Jacks," he said with a laugh. "You want to be a detective and I'll run the bookshop?"

I rolled my eyes and stepped off of the porch, on my way.

"Well, Marv is looking for me, apparently," I said as I walked down his sidewalk. "Maybe he's going to offer me your job?"

Jeremy laughed after me. "Good luck! I don't know what it is, but it's not *my* job. I'm irreplaceable, Jacks!"

"Yeah, yeah!" I waved at him over my shoulder.

CHAPTER SIX

Marv was sitting in the back corner booth of Harper's when I arrived minutes later to have lunch. Instead of checking in with Deb or Heidi, I skipped the process of having them seat me and headed straight to his table. I had no particular duty to report to Marv when I heard he was looking for me. I wasn't one of his officers, after all. However, I've always found that when certain citizens of Head Rock Harbor are looking for me, it's best to find out what they want as quickly as possible. Bite the bullet before the bullet bites you.

Chief Marv Bucksworth was so busy with his chicken fried steak platter that he didn't notice me approaching his table. When I slid into the seat across from him, he looked up, wide-eyed and intrigued by the sudden appearance of another human being. I gave him a small nod and placed my hands atop the table, lacing my fingers together.

Let another meeting begin.

"Marv," I said.

"Jackson," he said back. "I've been looking for you."

"That's what I hear," I replied. "And that's why I'm sitting across from you."

Marv cleared his throat and pushed back in the vinyl seat, a rude squeak emanating from beneath him. He gave me a fleeting, sheepish grin and cleared his throat. His dark tan uniform whispered from the starchiness as he shifted in his seat and the badge over his left breast glinted in the shaded bar light hanging over the table. His hat had to be sitting on the seat beside him—as it usually was when he sat down to eat.

Though he wasn't a much bigger man than Jeremy, he had a more commanding presence. It could have been the three decades he had on my friend, or it could have been his dark eyes that always seemed to see right through you. Likely, it was the fact that he was an older man in a uniform with a gun strapped to his hip. That usually makes someone appear commanding.

"Why'd you have to rile up Charlene Har—"

"I know nothing! Nothing!" I responded with my best Sergeant Schultz impression.

The schtick wouldn't have flown with anyone my age, but Marv was the perfect audience for the quip. Marv allowed the slightest of smiles, which permitted me to relax in my seat. Even if he was mad, he wasn't enraged. Jail time was not in my immediate future.

"She came into the office at the butt crack of dawn this morning talking about some auction idea the two of you have come up with," he said. "You wouldn't happen to know anything about that, would you?"

"Hold up, Marv," I said, raising my hands in defense. "Do you really think that was *our* idea?"

"Well, not particularly," he said as Deb approached our table, cutting him off.

"Well, well, well, look what the—"

"Cat dragged in," I said. "Philly cheesesteak and—"

"Rings," she said, finishing my thought as she walked away.

Marv took a moment to grin at my interaction with my mother, watching her walk away, before he turned his gaze back on me.

"Charlene seems to think you're bosom buddies, though," he said, picking up where he'd left off. "A team in this nonsense."

"She came to the shop last night," I explained, "talking about wanting to auction off Mr. Pemberton's stuff to get some clout for the HSBOA and I told her it was a bad idea."

"She didn't seem to recall it that way."

"Well," I sighed, continuing, "to get her to leave, I told her if you thought it was a good idea and the family agreed, I'd help. Well, I'd go with her to his house to make sure there was anything worth auctioning off first. She doesn't want to hire an estate appraiser and waste any money."

Marv's brow furrowed as he lifted his fork and cut into his chicken fried steak with the side of it. I waited for him to skewer the piece and get it into his mouth for a good chew.

"Well," he said around the bite of food, "I've been in touch with the family. Not about some cockamamie auction idea, but about his unfortunate passing."

I nodded along.

"They seem to be shell-shocked, as you can imagine," Marv continued as he ate his lunch, his eyes mostly on his food. "He's got one sister, little more than ten years older than him, and his elderly mother who's in some home in upstate New York. They moved with him from here when he went to the city, you know?"

A noncommittal grunt escaped my throat. I hadn't known, but there was no reason I would have known anything about Prescott Pemberton.

"They stayed behind," Marv continued. "Sister got married out there—widow now. Mother was living with her until she got too down in the health department to not need constant care, so the sister got her put in a home. I suppose they probably have bills what with the home and the sister being widowed. I don't know."

"I don't even really remember them," I said. "The Pembertons used to live here before his art career took off, or…?"

Marv was nodding and chewing.

"Yup. They got that big Victorian up there on the bluff?"

I nodded. I knew the house, but only from seeing it looking down on Head Rock Harbor from the bluff on the west side of town since before I could remember. There were only a dozen houses scattered along the steep hillside overlooking town, but only one of them was a Victorian. I could immediately picture it perfectly in my head.

"The Pembertons—mom and pop—bought that house back before you were born," Marv continued as he ate his lunch. "I guess you were probably a little thing when Prescott went off to college in New York. His father died sometime during those four years, so after he finished college and, I suppose got all artsy famous out there, he came and got his mom and sister and whisked 'em away. That Victorian was sitting empty until he came back a year ago.

Health reasons, his sister said. *New York wasn't good for him anymore*, or something like that."

"That explains why I know nothing about the guy."

Marv nodded along. "Well, by my calculations, his sister has gotta be pushing sixty if not stepping over it. Mom's gotta be in her eighties. Traveling back here to deal with their things would most likely be a burden."

Frowning to myself as I watched Marv chew contemplatively at his lip, I knew what was coming.

"I suppose it wouldn't hurt to check with them about the auction idea," he said with a sigh as he skewered the last bite from his plate. "They might actually appreciate it."

"You're killing me, Marv," I grumbled, but I managed to chuckle.

Chuckling along with me, he said, "Won't hurt you none to spend a few hours with Charlene in the house. You only promised to tell her if there was anything worth selling. After that, you're off the hook. Right?"

Reaching over, I flicked the corner of his plate with my finger, a "ding" resonating loudly. Then I slid from the booth and stood next to the table. Marv coughed out a chuckle as he looked up at me and finished chewing his bite of food.

"One day," I said, "I'm going to learn to keep my fat mouth shut."

A bark of laughter escaped Marv's throat.

"We'll see about that," he said. "I'm surprised you didn't know more about Mr. Pemberton. He's one of your people after all."

"My people?"

"Gay," Marv gestured vaguely.

"I didn't see him at the last conference," I said, blandly. "And I'm not signed up for the newsletter."

Marv chuckled and waved me off. "I'll figure what's what with the family and let Charlene know what the final verdict is. Then she—"

"Will assault me at the shop again. Got it. Tell Gladys I said 'hello,' okay?"

"Will do."

As I turned to walk away, Marv said nothing else, but he was chuckling—either at my comment about Charlene assaulting me or him needing to tell his wife "hi" for me. I slid into a seat at one of the four tops automatically, intending to wait for Deb to bring out my cheesesteak and rings. However, after looking around the dimly lit bar, I realized it was too early in the day to be sitting in a dark bar, eating greasy food.

"Deb!" I hollered. "Can you make mine to go?"

Beau's head popped out of the passthrough to the kitchen, a confused look on his face. When he saw me, he smiled and nodded.

"She went out back for a smoke, Jackson," he said. "I'll make it to go for you."

"Great," I said. "Thanks."

Abandoning the table, I went over to the passthrough to collect my order from Beau Robison. Impressively handsome—like his brother Sawyer—I collected my lunch order without somehow stumbling over my words or drooling at the sight of the man. I don't think I'm better than anyone else, but getting googly-eyed over the handsome cook in my mother's restaurant like every woman in town was something I simply couldn't abide.

I handed him a five-dollar bill as a tip—honestly, it wasn't to garner his favor—and headed out. I never had to pay for my meals at Harper's since my mother owned and ran the place, but I always left a tip for whoever gave me my food—if they allowed it. It only seemed fair considering I was essentially a mooch.

Aimlessly, I walked through town since I had no other plans for the day. No chores or errands were begging for my attention, and while still a bit chilly, we were having one of our warmer early spring days in Head Rock Harbor. Which was where I eventually found myself. The harbor. Without meaning to, I'd walked from Harper's all the way back across town, past my shop, down Harbor Street, and to the harbor itself.

With nothing better to do than commit to the location where I'd found myself, I sat down at one of the picnic tables close to the grassy shore, not far from the boat ramp. I did my best to ignore the fact that I was sitting mere yards away from where a man's life had ended. Unwrapping the cheesesteak and rings that I pulled out of the paper bag helped distract me from the thought.

I'm not really a superstitious man or a believer in the afterlife—none of that hocus pocus or spiritual nonsense—but death does make a place feel...*different.* Knowing a man had seen the last seconds of his life in the general vicinity made the picnic area in the harbor feel chillier than anywhere else in town. Somehow, I managed to ignore that feeling as I dug into my sandwich, and within a few bites, I'd completely forgotten about Prescott Pemberton.

The green ashes and American elms in the park looked as though they were getting ready to bloom for the spring. The silver maples, bur oaks, cottonwoods, and hackberry trees that trimmed the shore of the Mississippi looked like they weren't far behind. Soon, the birds would be chirping. The water would be warmer and more people would be out swimming, boating, fishing, and life, not death, would fill the harbor again.

I finished up my cheesesteak and rings, throwing all of my trash back into the paper bag. Like a good citizen, I deposited the bag of trash in the metal barrel near the top of the ramp that led down into the harbor. As I stepped up onto the ramp, the toe of my sneaker hooked under something, and before I knew it, I was tumbling face first towards the concrete ramp.

Fortunately, I was able to catch myself and avoid the embarrassment—and pain—of a faceplant onto the boat ramp. With its divots and unfinished roughness, it would have made a beautiful pattern on my face. I winced as I righted myself, checking out the palms of my hands. A bit of gravel to be picked away and a few superficial scratches, but otherwise I had survived.

Cursing under my breath, but mostly chuckling at my clumsiness, I got my footing and began looking around for what had tripped me. My eyes landed on a thick slat of wood that had been painted white, numbers written along the length of it. After a moment, I realized I was looking at the flood gauge. It had worked its way out of the ground and had been wedged under the lip of the ramp—probably with the help of the wind during a particularly gusty night.

Nothing more than a two by four painted white with black numbers painted along the side, the flood gauge was a simple tool used by citizens to see how high the river rose during times the Mississippi flooded. I'd missed the great flood of 1993, but I was alive for the floods that affected Head Rock Harbor in 2011 and 2014. The great flood of 2019 affected our little burg as well. So, the flood gauge was used more frequently than one might imagine.

I pulled the gauge out from under the lip of the ramp and righted it. With no tools to help me, I did my best to wedge it back into its earthen hole at the top of the ramp. My hands were dirty and a little scratched up when I was done, but I'd done my good deed for the day as a citizen of Head Rock Harbor.

After making a mental note to myself to tell Linda Wagner to get someone to repaint the chipped and faded gauge, I stepped up on the ramp. Having been such a great citizen—if only for a moment—I decided to stop by Pain for a pastry on my way back home.

CHAPTER SEVEN

"It seems unreasonable to me that all of these homes got built up here," Charlene was yammering away as she slid the key in the lock, "but I wasn't here when they were planning the layout of the town, was I?"

"Well—"

"Who even builds homes up on a bluff for crying out loud?" She continued her tirade as she unlocked the front door and pushed it wide. "The drive up here alone! Can you imagine having to walk up to these houses before there were cars?"

"I think that—"

"Leave it to the rich to come up with such ostentatious displays for their homes," she said, shaking her head as she stepped inside of the house.

I gave up. Charlene was going to perform her monologue about the houses on the bluff from beginning to end without interruption, and there was nothing I could do about it. Interrupting her monologue wasn't really important to me anyway. Even though I did want to explain to Charlene that she, along with everyone else in town, was technically incorrect in referring to the geological feature as a "bluff."

A bluff is a rounded steep cliff or bank, typically bordering a river or beach of some kind. While the Mississippi can easily be seen from any of the houses on the geographical feature all of the citizens of Head Rock Harbor refer to as The Bluff—it's really a steep hill that's further inland. A winding, twisting, snake-like road that is especially treacherous in winter leads up and around the hill to the homes scattered about it.

All of the homes on the hillside that overlook Head Rock Harbor below are of the nicer variety. Victorians, Mid-Century Modern, Après Ski Lodge, and a few large Craftsman homes look out among the trees and boulders. Bluff Road, leading up the hillside, is a beautifully paved and maintained road, and the driveways branching off randomly to the homes on the hillside are comprised of cobblestone and brick. Rich people have the money and time to maintain brick and cobblestone driveways, I suppose.

Needless to say, the fact that Prescott Pemberton owned a Victorian home up on The Bluff was not all that surprising. A guy who ran off to New York City with his family to become hot stuff in the art world obviously had to have some money. Normal people don't leave smalltown Iowa to chase their artistic dreams without a backup plan, after all. The Victorian Charlene was leading me into was a good backup plan.

"So," Charlene said, continuing her yammering as I stepped across the threshold, "as I was saying on the drive up here—"

I nearly cringed, thinking of the ride up to Prescott Pemberton's house. Charlene had called Thursday evening to tell me that Prescott's family had been ecstatic at the idea of the city of Head Rock Harbor helping them take care of the sale of Prescott's things. So, Charlene had informed me that she would be picking me up at the shop on Sunday after she got out of church so we could go up to the house. She hadn't given me a second to protest, instead hanging up as soon as the words had left her mouth.

Now, with key in hand from Marv, Charlene was letting us into the house of a dead man. All so we could assess the contents of his life and decide if it was good enough for strangers to poke through and offer a bid. The whole thing seemed distasteful to me. Without his family involved, it felt like grave robbing—even if the strangers poking through Prescott's things would be paying actual money to take his things.

Then again, all I had to do was fulfill my promise to give an assessment of the belongings. After that, I was no longer involved. I had not promised to commit any more energy or time—or emotions—to the process.

"—the artwork, obviously, will be the most important thing to assess. Of course, in a house like this, I'm sure there's bound to be some antiques, too."

Closing the front door and locking out the howling wind that was blowing off the river and up the hillside, I shivered. Charlene squinted when I found the light switch on the wall and flipped on the foyer light. The murky darkness of the entryway lit up golden, exposing the darkly stained oak wainscoting and Juniper green wallpaper. The dark oak floorboards underfoot practically shone in the golden light.

"Well," Charlene stated breathlessly, "isn't this a surprise?"

"Surprise?" I asked, my eyes taking in the wood detailing around the doorway leading into the parlor to our right.

"A bachelor? Living here? Immaculate."

"Not all bachelors are pigs, Charlene," I said with a chuckle, moving farther into the house.

The floorboards creaked faintly underfoot, but not from lack of maintenance. Straight ahead a wooden, carpeted staircase led to the second floor. All oak stained dark and carved meticulously by what could only be Heaven's carpenters. A double-wide doorway at the base of the stairs led off the entry to the left and into a dining room with the same impressive wainscoting, wallpaper, and floorboards.

Glancing into the dining room, a swinging door led off the side into an unknown room, which I could only assume was the kitchen. If we traveled further down the entry hall, past the staircase, I assumed we'd find another entry into the kitchen. Looking into both the parlor and dining room, I saw that all of the windows had their heavy drapes pulled shut. Little light was able to sneak through, so the house felt cavernous and murky.

"Immaculate," Charlene said again. "But still needs a woman's touch."

I had no idea what to say to that, so I decided to be polite.

"Opening some of these drapes would probably make a world of difference," I said. "A little sunlight does wonders for any home."

"Hm." Charlene put a finger to her chin and turned slowly, taking in the entryway around us. "Do you think we'll be here long enough to bother?"

Charlene thought this over only a moment.

"Maybe for the auction. No need to go through opening all the drapes and windows now," she answered herself.

"Okay," I said, glad to know that I would not be present for any possible auction that took place. "Where do you want to start?"

Before she could open her mouth to lay out her plan, the front door whipped open behind us, a belch of cold river air slapping against our backs. Charlene and I both spun to see who had opened the front door, our hair dancing freely on our heads. A stocky woman, short and sturdy, marched across the threshold, her head down against the wind. The yellow windbreaker she had thrown over her dark argyle sweater and jeans flapped mercilessly in the wind.

The two of us stared at the strange woman in awe as she entered the house like a whirlwind—*actual wind included*—and spun to slam the door behind her. Huffing and pink in the face, she turned and pushed back the hood of her jacket, jumping slightly at the sight of us. I wanted to point out that we were the ones who should be startled, but I figured finding out who the woman was first would be more important.

"Oh!" she exclaimed. "Chief Bucksworth told me that you two would be here. I don't know why you startled me."

Charlene and I exchanged a glance.

"Of course, I guess I didn't expect to run directly into you, either," the woman said with a chuckle. "I'm Marshelle."

When Charlene and I showed no signs of recognition, she continued.

"*Marshelle Martin?*" she asked. "Prescott's assistant. *Former* assistant?"

Charlene looked at me again. Someone had to take charge.

"I'm sorry, Ms. Martin," I said, extending my hand. "Marv—Chief Bucksworth didn't tell us that Prescott had an assistant."

Marshelle Martin graciously accepted my hand and gave it a shake. Charlene finally offered her hand and they exchanged pleasantries as well.

"Well," Marshelle sighed, "I suppose it's not so important any more. Me having been his assistant, I mean. My services are, obviously, no longer needed."

"I'm sorry to hear that," I said. "I mean, both Prescott's death and the loss of your job. I'm sure there's something else in Head Rock Harbor for you...?"

Marshelle Martin laughed as though this was the craziest thing she'd ever heard.

"I'm going back to New York as soon as I can! I just have to swing by the Inn. I don't care what anybody says. It's time to leave. I've had about all I can take after being out here with Prescott," she said.

Laughing for a moment, a look flashed across her face and Marshelle turned bright pink. Apparently, what she had said to two citizens of Head Rock Harbor had dawned on her. Sputtering and straightening her windbreaker to buy time, her eyes flicked everywhere in the room but at us. I hadn't been offended—but it was amusing watching her scramble to correct her manners.

"What I mean—"

"It's okay," I said with a chuckle. "Head Rock Harbor must be pretty boring compared to New York City."

Marshelle gave me a small, apologetic smile.

"Less murders and overall crime definitely make it less exciting," Charlene stated snippily behind me.

I shot Charlene a frown, but didn't respond to her comment. Marshelle's face found a new shade of blush to display.

"Did Marv send you over to help us?" I asked, changing the subject.

"Oh!" Marshelle was flitting about in her windbreaker again, her hands groping her pockets. "He asked me to bring this by today…"

Charlene and I waited patiently as Marshelle's hands slid in and out of the numerous pockets in her windbreaker, then finally, her jeans pockets. When she pulled her hand out of her right hip pocket, a glint of gold caught my eye.

"He asked me to drop this off," Marshelle said, extending her hand. "I won't be needing it anymore, so, it's best to leave it here or give it to one of you. I drove down to the police department to give it to him, but he sent me right back up here."

A glance at her palm confirmed what I suspected. A house key. When Marshelle pushed her hand at me, I held my hands up and stepped aside. Charlene stepped up and took the key from Marshelle, slipping it from the palm of her hand into her own front hip pocket.

"I suppose a spare key will be important while we're inventorying the house and planning the auction," Charlene said vaguely.

"Yes, well," Marshelle sighed deeply, looking around, "I'll miss the place. And Prescott. But I'm glad to be going home. I've already cleaned out the fridge, so there's not much to eat if you get hungry, but you might find a few nibbles in the pantry if you're desperate while you're here. I've packed up and loaded all of my belongings from my room, so everything else should be fair game."

"I think we'll be fine," Charlene said snootily, then turned on her heels and marched off towards the back of the house, past the stairs.

Frowning, I watched her disappear behind the stairs, presumably into the kitchen. I shrugged and turned to face Marshelle, trying to smile warmly. She had to be grieving after all.

"I'm sorry," I said. "She's…Charlene."

Marshelle chuckled. "I'm from New York. The Iowa Frost doesn't faze me."

I joined her in chuckling. "I'm sorry about your employer—and friend, I suppose? I didn't know him, but I never heard anything bad about him, either."

"Nature of the beast," Marshelle said. "When we moved back here after his health got so bad in New York, he became a homebody. A shut-in, really. He didn't like going out and he didn't like letting anyone in—except people he knew, of course."

"Of course."

"He didn't even like for me to leave," she said, shaking her head mirthfully. "He didn't like to draw attention to himself or his doings. We had to have practically everything delivered. Groceries, his art supplies, you name it."

"Sounds…lonely."

"Well, I do well alone, I suppose," Marshelle smiled, the pink returning to her face. "And Prescott had his *visitors* from time to time."

The tone and my context clues let me know what Marshelle meant by "visitors," so I said nothing and only smiled at the comment. Quiet grew pervasive in the entryway between us when there was nothing left to be said about the deceased. I didn't know him, and Marshelle wasn't going to share more.

"I suppose this is it," she said with another sigh. "Off on another adventure."

"Exciting times," I agreed neutrally, following her to the door.

When I pulled the door open, a gust of wind blew into the house, but the wind had calmed down considerably in the last few minutes. Our hair danced lazily on our heads instead of twirling crazily. As she stepped over the threshold, Marshelle turned to me, sadness marking the corners of her eyes.

"It's just so sad," she said. "After all these years, and then he…well. I suppose the illness is lifelong, isn't it?"

"Prescott?" I asked. "What *was* the reason for his bad health in New York? If it's not rude of me to ask."

"Oh," Marshelle said, waving me off, "not that. He was just weak, a bit dizzy at times, always sleepy. Had sporadic headaches. I told him to get checked out by a doctor but he just wanted to come back to Head Rock Harbor and rest up. He thought the river air would miraculously cure him or something. He said life had *caught up to him* in New York."

"It is nice here. It's definitely quieter than New York."

I glanced over her head to the river in the distance below us.

"But it was the alcoholism, you know," she said. "He'd been clean for so long. I really hate that he lost his battle."

"Oh," I said, suddenly sad. "I wasn't...well, I'm sorry to hear that."

"Ten years," Marshelle said, shaking her head. "It's funny how the disease of addiction works. Ten years clean, then you jump off the deep end. Typically, you just scrape 'em up, get rid of the trigger, and the recovery begins again. Not this time. Oh, gosh. I'm going to get weepy here."

I started to say something, I wasn't sure what, but Marshelle gestured to leave it be. So, I did.

"Thank you and...*Charlene*...for doing this for his sister. She's so busy with Mrs. Pemberton that it would have practically killed her to come back here and do this herself."

Smiling, I said, "We're happy to help. Charlene will make sure everything goes smoothly."

Marshelle gave me a smile, stepped back, looked up at the house, grinning happily, then her eyes were on me again. She gave me a small nod of her head, but said nothing as she turned and dashed across the driveway to the little silver Toyota she'd somehow driven up the hillside to return her key to Prescott's house.

As I watched her drive off into the distance, I found myself frowning. Not that I was heartless, but Prescott's death hadn't affected me greatly. People accidentally die all the time. Knowing that he had died because he'd lost a battle with alcoholism somehow made it more tragic. If he hadn't taken a drink...which led to many more drinks that night...he would still be alive. And I wouldn't be in his house with Charlene planning to pick through his things like a couple of vultures.

I gave a final wave to the disappearing car in the distance and walked back into the house, closing the door behind me.

"Charlene?" I hollered down the hallway leading to the back of the house.

After a few moments with no answer, I walked through the dark dining room to what I assumed was the kitchen door. Swinging the door, sunlight assaulted me. I'd found the kitchen, and it appeared to be the only room downstairs that did not have drapes. In fact, the kitchen was downright cheerful compared to the rest of the house I'd seen already.

Instead of dark woods and wallpaper, the kitchen was yellow paint, glimmering white tiles, and white cabinets with squeaky clean glass inserts. Though I was happy to see that some part of Prescott's house wasn't gloomy, my mission to find Charlene had failed. Furrowing my brow in frustration, I walked through the kitchen to the other swinging door that led into the hallway.

I found myself at the back of the stairs, as I had expected, and I was shrouded in the gloom again. Though the front hall light wasn't exceptionally bright, the golden glow allowed me to see that the other rooms downstairs—a half bathroom and a den-like room—were unoccupied. Confused at how Charlene had simply disappeared, I walked to the base of the stairs and laid a hand on the newel post.

"*Charlene?*" I hollered up the stairs.

Unless she had slipped out the backdoor, there was nowhere else Charlene could have gone, though I hadn't seen her go up the stairs, either. I started up the stairs, two at a time, preparing to holler her name again, when she finally answered. I couldn't quite make out what Charlene had said, but it was clear her voice was coming from the second floor.

Upstairs, I marched down a hallway equally as gloomy as the entry hall, peeking my head into each room, looking for

Charlene. Finally, at the end of the hallway, I found her in what had to have been Prescott's art studio. Two walls of the corner room were lined with windows, allowing the sunlight to pour inside. The lack of drapes or window coverings meant lots of natural light—perfect for painting by, or so I'd heard from other artists before.

"Well," Charlene said, throwing her hands in the air when I stepped through the door, "I found the art. Such as it is."

"Good," I replied, giving the room a once over.

Drop cloths splotched with a variety of hues lined the wood floor. The walls were bare and blindingly white. A pile of discarded—or possibly used—supplies were stacked in one corner, along with a white towel that had been tossed on the pile, obviously as yet unused to wipe up messes. A set of clothes that Prescott obviously wore while painting was topped haphazardly in a heap. Off to the side, a half-bath was available, its door open. A single easel with a stretched canvas stood in the center of the room, and Charlene was standing before it, frowning. I walked across the expansive room and rounded the easel to look at it with Charlene. My frown joined hers.

"It's…not much," I said.

The canvas had little more than a few splotches of paint splattered upon it. It was impossible to tell what Prescott would have even been thinking about painting. On the floor, between the three legs of the easel sat his dry artist's palette, a few closed tubes of oil paint, and a brush that had been cleaned thoroughly. It looked as though he hadn't painted in many days—even before his death. Whatever project he had started obviously had been uninspiring.

"Prescott Pemberton's final painting," Charlene sighed. "I suppose we could call it 'abstract' and still auction it off."

"Don't be a ghoul, Charlene," I said.

She chuckled.

"Well, if this isn't odd enough," she said, "I don't see any more artwork around here."

Confused, I turned around, following her gaze around the room. Charlene was right. There weren't any finished canvases leaning against the wall drying. None dried and stacked. None hanging on the walls. The only artwork was what was on the easel—and it wasn't even artwork, as far as I was concerned. Rattlesnatches could have painted something similar if I dipped his paws in paint first.

"That's odd," I said. "He must keep his finished artwork somewhere else."

"I hope so," Charlene clicked her tongue, "or this might have been a waste of our time. Or his little assistant cleared out more than her room and the fridge."

I frowned, but said nothing. I knew in the back of my mind that Charlene had really only wanted to get access to Prescott Pemberton's paintings. *A dead artist is a popular artist,* after all. But I hadn't wanted to believe it. Helping Prescott's family deal with the belongings and house after his untimely death was important, too.

"We'll have to look around," I said, finally.

"Let's do that," Charlene turned her nose up. "It stinks in here, anyway."

As soon as she mentioned it, I noticed the smell. Instinctively, I brought a hand to my nose and covered it. The smell wasn't strong, but it was an unpleasant fishy aroma.

"What is that?" I asked.

"I don't know," Charlene said. "But we'll have to air this room out before we let people traipse through here. No one will want to buy the place if it smells like...*fish*."

Nodding, I agreed.

"Let's go look for his artwork," Charlene gestured towards the door. "After that we can look at the furniture and any possible antiques hidden about the place. Hopefully, this won't have been for nothing. I swear—if that assistant took anything from this house that wasn't hers, I'm going to tell Prescott's family to have her arrested and charged. I'll hunt her down myself!"

"I'm sure she didn't take anything that wasn't hers, Charlene."

"You never know about people. Everyone is crazy nowadays!"

Not pleased with Charlene's attitude, but wanting to get away from the smell, I followed her back out of the studio.

CHAPTER EIGHT

Dinner was bubbling gently on the stove top as I stirred it gently and held my cell phone to my ear with my free hand. When I'd clicked on Jeremy's contact to call him, I hadn't actually expected him to pick up. Though, when he did, I hid my surprise as best I could.

"*What's up?*" he asked.

"Goulash will be ready in about twenty minutes," I said. "You in or out?"

Jeremy hemmed and hawed for a moment as I stirred the mixture in the pot.

"This isn't your mother's goulash," I added. "It's actually seasoned."

"*Tempting.*" Jeremy laughed. "*It's not even goulash. It's noodles and meat and tomatoes.*"

"That's fair," I said as I stirred. "Except this is the Midwest. You coming to eat Sunday dinner or what? I've got beers, a cake from Pain—okay, most of a cake from Pain, I ate some yesterday—and the movie of your choice."

Jeremy chuckled.

"*Gotta pass this time, Jacks,*" he said. "*Got a date.*"

I was disappointed, but I understood. It was the nature of the beast. Men and "dating" were important to my best friend. Even the Midwestern-style staple meal of goulash couldn't keep him from following his nature.

"You're getting lucky lately," I said as I prodded the concoction with a wooden spoon. "That's nearly every night this week. Or every night, maybe?"

"*Not lucky,*" Jeremy said. "*Same guy. Once I hook 'em, they keep coming back for more, my friend. He's waiting for me at his place, as a matter of fact.*"

"His place?" I asked.

"*He stays at the Inn.*"

"This the day laborer guy?"

"*One and the same.*"

"How long is he going to be in town?" I asked. "I won't bother begging you to come to dinner again until then."

"*Har-har,*" Jeremy replied. "*I don't know. I don't care. He'll eventually be gone or I'll get bored. Just let me have fun!*"

Laughing, I decided to give Jeremy a break.

"*Hey,*" Jeremy asked quickly, "*weren't you and Charlene supposed to be at the Pemberton place today?*"

"Yeah," I said. "We were."

"*Huh. I must have missed you. Marv told me that y'all would be there, but it was quiet as a tomb when I got there.*"

"When did you show up?" I asked as I stopped prodding the pot and partially covered it with the lid.

Once the noodles were fully cooked, I'd be ready to eat. I stepped over to the fridge and pulled out a soda to have with my dinner.

"*Three-ish?*"

"Yeah," I said as I slid into a seat at the kitchen table, "we were gone by then. There wasn't as much to look at as Charlene had hoped."

"*I kind of figured that,*" Jeremy said. "*I checked to make sure the place was locked up and all the lights were off. For all its beauty, the Pembertons sure didn't waste any money decking out the place, huh?*"

That statement made me think about the phone I had pressed to my ear. With a lack of artwork to catalog, Charlene had insisted I take pictures of anything she thought might be worth something—mostly furniture—so I could give it all a good look later, then let her know what to expect when it came to having an auction. My hopes weren't high, I but I figured I'd examine the pictures more closely over dinner.

"I wasn't super impressed," I said.

"*Well,*" Jeremy said, "*we'll catch up soon. Promise.*"

"All right. Bye, Germ."

"*Smooches, Jacks!*"

Laughing to myself at Jeremy's ridiculousness, I waited for the call to end, then flipped over to the photos app to check out the pictures I'd taken from earlier in the day. The photos I'd taken of Prescott's studio—such as it was—and all of the upstairs rooms were good. Without heavy drapes blocking out the natural light, I could clearly see everything that might be of interest in an auction.

The downstairs photos were another situation entirely. Since we hadn't opened the drapes, the parlor, dining room, den, and bathroom looked garish in the light of my phone's flash. The kitchen was the only downstairs room that looked pleasant in the downstairs photos. However, natural light or not, it was obvious that any auction would not result in record profits for the Pembertons.

As I looked over the photos, I tried to think of any place in the house we hadn't checked for artwork. Charlene and I had opened all closets, all hidey-holes, looked behind furniture, checked the attic, and searched for a nonexistent basement before giving up. Prescott had no finished work in his studio, hanging on the walls, or hidden away. We even checked the shed and detached garage before leaving, but that only introduced us to dusty, unused garden equipment and an '82 Oldsmobile that probably hadn't been driven in twenty years.

Considering all things, the furniture all seemed to be made of solid wood—if not antiques—and would probably sell easily. However, we were looking more at a garage sale situation than an auction—which I hated to have to tell Charlene. If she and the Pembertons were smart, they would have us remove any important personal items, ship them off to New York, and sell the house "as-is." The house itself was beautiful and simply needed a loving touch to become glorious. It would even make a beautiful bed and breakfast if someone had the entrepreneurial spirit in town.

I made a mental note to ask Lila Westbrook if she would be interested in expanding her empire. If opening a second inn didn't appeal to her, it was possibly she would know someone who would be interested. People in an industry tend to know other people's plans in the same industry, so Lila would be a great place to start. It was possible that no one in town would be interested, but contacting a realtor for a regular sale would be easy.

"*Meow.*"

I was shaken from my thoughts by Rattlesnatches mewling at me and rubbing the length of his side along my calf. When I reached down to pet him, he leapt from the floor up to the countertop next to the stove.

"Get off the counter," I said. "You know you're not allowed up—"

When I turned in my seat to admonish Rattlesnatches, my eyes were immediately drawn to the smoke belching out from under the lid of the partially closed pot. Leaping to my feet, I stepped over to the stove, pushed the goulash off of the burner, and whipped off the lid. I simultaneously turned off the burner and plunged the wooden spoon into the stew.

Burnt.

Noodles had already blackened and stuck to the bottom of the pot. As I pushed the wooden spoon through the half-burned pot of stew, I could tell that maybe the top half was salvageable. If I could get over the burnt taste the bottom half had imparted on it. I pushed the pot to the back of the stove in defeat. I wasn't going to eat burnt food simply to be frugal.

"Next time," I turned to look at Rattlesnatches, "remind me before it starts smoking."

"*Meow.*" He gazed up at me with his coppery eyes.

"Yeah, yeah," I said. "Get off the counter."

Rattlesnatches dropped softly from the counter to the floor before sauntering over to my bed at the other end of my apartment. He leapt up, pawed at the covers, circled a few times, then curled up into a tight ball, fast asleep. To live the life of a pampered cat. If one believes in reincarnation, and human is not an option for the next life, pampered cat is a great next choice.

Without a second thought, I grabbed my keys and wallet from the counter, my jacket from the hook by the apartment door, and made my way downstairs. At the front door of the shop, I lifted the light switch cover and turned the lights off, then let myself out. I didn't want anyone stopping by, seeing the lights, and assuming the shop was open. I'd never hear the end of complaints the following day if a customer stopped by, the lights were on, but the door was locked.

Minutes later, I was shuffling into Munchies. The sun had nearly dipped below the horizon and the first stars were peeking out of the navy blanket overhead. Shirley and Lardell had found themselves with a busier than usual Sunday evening, so Shirley and I barely had time to make niceties before she took my order and zipped away. Even for having their dining room full, Lardell had my pork tenderloin, fries, ranch, and cole slaw ready in record time.

Without Shirley to chat with over my meal, I ate in silence, giving a kind nod to people at other tables I knew from around town. I pulled out my phone and zipped through the pictures I'd taken at the Pembertons once more. It became obvious, not that I'd really needed to check again, that there wasn't going to be much to auction for the family. Prescott not having produced any artwork was a real shock—and a huge disappointment for Charlene. When we'd left the house earlier in the day, I could practically feel her annoyance. The lift she'd given me back to the bookstore had been tense and mostly silent.

Sighing, I popped out of the photos app and pulled up my search engine. Before his death, I'd never really known anything about Prescott Pemberton; I hadn't known he existed. I was uncertain that searching for him online would produce any results about his art. However, I assumed that if he'd had any bit of success in New York City, there had to be an article or two about him somewhere. Maybe even a few pictures of him at galleries and art exhibitions.

Pleasantly surprised by my search, I found several articles pertaining to Prescott Pemberton's time in New York. As expected, most were about openings at art galleries, the selling of artwork, the typical things one would expect. He even had a Wikipedia page that seemed to be updated regularly by enthusiastic fans of his work. Apparently, news of his death had made its way to the fans who did the updating.

I switched from search hits to images and found that a few dozen of Prescott's paintings were available on the page. Most were images posted by art galleries that had sold his work or had exhibitions for him. My brow furrowed as I took in the images. They were nothing like the splotches of paint on the canvas in his home studio.

Though I'm no art expert, I would have said that Prescott Pemberton was a post-Impressionist inspired painter. The painter that immediately came to mind to compare him to was Henri de Toulouse-Lautrec. With his colorful impressionist interpretations of interiors and the characters that inhabited them, it was the best comparison I could make. I could have easily seen Prescott designing posters advertising La Goulue dancing the Can-Can at the Moulin Rouge. The painting—if you could call it that—on the easel in his home studio didn't hold a candle to what I'd found online.

Looking at the paintings broke my heart for two reasons. One, it was obvious that coming home to Head Rock Harbor had not healed or inspired Prescott. In fact, it might have produced some type of artist's block. Two, I felt even worse for Charlene. If we had run across paintings like those I'd found when searching Prescott online, she would have had an auction worth promoting to all of the large cities nearby. With what we currently had, we'd be lucky if anybody in town bothered driving up the hill to see what was on offer.

Prescott Pemberton, for what it was worth, left a legacy of beautiful paintings in his lifetime. As a dead artist, however, there were no undiscovered or unsold paintings to augment his legacy. Prescott's life—like most people's—had come to an end with a whimper instead of a bang.

CHAPTER NINE

"He's quite possibly my *favorite* literary detective!"

Rattlesnatches had draped himself around my neck and fallen asleep—much to the delight of my customers—and Heidi Cook was chewing my ear off as I worked the checkout counter at the shop. She'd stopped by the shop for some late morning browsing before her shift at Harper's.

Much to my delight, Monday was the beginning of Spring Break for many of the schools in the area. I'd seen a record number of sales on Monday, and Tuesday morning was flying by so quickly my head was spinning. Tourists were in town for the river life and other attractions Head Rock Harbor had to offer. Extra people in town meant extra books being sold.

Head Rock Harbor Books has much less to offer than a big-name bookstore in a bigger city. We don't even have a coffee and snack bar. However, something about a smalltown bookstore makes people want buy a book while on vacation. It's the novelty and uniqueness of the experience, I suppose. *Quaint little bookstore in a quaint little town—the owner even lives above the store!* People from big cities romanticize small town businesses in the way travelers to foreign countries go wild over local wildlife. However, instead of wanting to squeeze a koala until it can't breathe, people throw money at small businesses like loons.

Needless to say, I was going to have to do an extra inventory session and I wasn't even sure if I would be able to close at lunch time as I typically did on Tuesdays. In fact, if the pattern continued, Wednesday's early closing was up in the air as well. Not that I minded staying open if people were buying books, but I did enjoy my short days.

"You might not be the only one who feels that way," I said as I rang up another shopper. "I'm completely out of Harrison Garner books at the moment. I sold my last one an hour ago."

"Oh!" Heidi jerked. "I'm glad I got a copy of his latest when they came in!"

"That'll be forty-nine sixty-six, please," I nodded at the card reader while making eye contact with the patron.

The out-of-towner who had just purchased two hardbacks—crime novels—reached into her pocketbook for a card. She was trying to pay for her purchases and keep up with the conversation Heidi was forcing me to participate in while I worked.

"Detective Randy Melton is the *best*! He's my book boyfriend!" Heidi pronounced as the lady at the counter went to put her card in the reader and missed. "I'm halfway through the latest book and I'll be dying for the next one when I'm done. Why does Harrison Garner take so long to release new books?"

The lady trying to check out was pink-cheeked and had corrected her aim, plunging her credit card into the reader with precision. A second later, it beeped and she retrieved her card. The register finalized the sale with a few beeps and whirs.

"Well," I said to Heidi as I pulled the receipt for the customer, "he's been releasing one or two a year for—"

"That's not good enough!" Heidi cut me off as I slipped the books and receipt into a bag for the customer. "He's got to find a way to write faster!"

I laughed as I handed the customer her bag, thanked her, and turned to Heidi.

"The books wouldn't be so good if he just pumped out stories, right?" I asked.

"Well—"

"So, you'll just have to wait until—"

"I heard," Heidi stopped me as another customer stepped up to the register with a stack of books, "that this might be the last one!"

As if time itself had gone on the fritz, it was if all life in the shop ceased to continue. Every townie and tourist that was in Head Rock Harbor Books stopped what they were doing to turn and look at the check-out counter. Frowning, and a bit embarrassed at being put on the spot, I began scanning the barcodes on the stack of books in front of me.

"Who told you that?" I grumbled.

Everyone in the shop seemed to be listening in, waiting for any gossip about Harrison Garner's writing career.

"*Your friend* Detective Jeremy Morris—that's who!" Heidi proclaimed, as if she had caught me in the center of a scandal.

Obviously, if Jeremy knew something about the publishing world, he'd heard it from me. And I, as a bookseller, obviously knew all the gossip about everyone in the publishing world. If Jeremy heard something about books, he'd obviously heard it from me, and if I had said it, it was gospel. That's how smalltown gossip begins and ends. Without facts or reason.

"I didn't tell Jeremy that. It doesn't matter if he's my friend," I said, shrugging it off as I rang up the books.

The tourist buying the stack of books was watching my conversation with Heidi with great interest. Obviously, she was a Harrison Garner fan, too.

"No," Heidi smiled smugly, "but he heard it from Lila. And *she* heard it from you."

A few gasps rose from the stacks in the store. Rolling my eyes, I completed the sale for the tourist waiting on their stack of books, before turning my full attention to Heidi.

"I merely said that I'd *heard* that might be true," I said, raising my voice to be heard by the entire store. "I don't know for certain. Harrison Garner is going to do what Harrison Garner wants to do."

"But—"

"And I have no idea if this will be his last or not," I continued. "However, if I hear anything definitive, I'll be sure to let everyone know. Okay?"

Heidi, flustered at my refusal to truly answer her question about Harrison Garner's personal decision of whether or not to write more books, stomped her foot. With her arms lacing over her chest, she turned her nose up at me.

"Well," she said, searching for words, "tell Jeremy to stop picking up all the cute guys that come through town!"

I, along with a few other townies, laughed.

"He swoops in before anyone else can!" Heidi marched towards the door. Halfway out the door, she turned for one last jab. "It's a new one every week with him!"

Then she was gone. I was still laughing when the next stack of books was heaved up onto the counter in front of me. Rattlesnatches yawned and sniffed the air gently, then went back to sleep around my shoulders.

I spent the rest of the morning helping customer select books, ringing up stacks of books, accepting payments, straightening displays and shelves, and providing a resting place for Rattlesnatches. He didn't move from around my shoulders all morning—which delighted and amused my patrons. Even the townies who were used to him.

Fortunately, by the time lunch was drawing close, things were dying down in the shop. With the arrival of the dining hour, the townies knew that I would want to close up shop, and the tourists were in search of a midday meal. Throughout the morning I'd suggested Munchies and Harper's to numerous people. We had a few fancier restaurants in town, but they were my two favorites.

If a customer had looked like they were looking for a fine dining experience, I would have suggested The Dock to them. It was a nicer restaurant on the north end of town, settled on a grassy expanse of land just a few yards from the shore of the Mississippi. With beautiful views—especially at night—amazing dishes to choose from at lunch time, and an available prix fixe menu for the evening service, it was probably the nicest restaurant in town.

However, though it might have been biased of me, none of the customers who asked for recommendations looked like they were wanting to drop beaucoup bucks on lunch.

Throughout the week, if more customers asked about fine dining at night, I'd drop the name for them. Until someone looked like they were looking for an elevated dining experience, I was going to stick with my usual recommendations. Besides, Head Rock Harbor is not that big. You can practically see from one end to the other. Most likely, all of the tourists would come across The Dock at some point or another anyway.

"So," I said, standing at the locked front door at lunch time, "it's a nice day. Do you want to go for a walk?"

I looked down at Rattlesnatches, who had leapt from my shoulders to sit quietly on his haunches at my feet. A soft mewling escaped his throat as he blinked lazily up at me.

"All right," I said. "But no tree climbing this time."

Rattlesnatches said nothing, so I assumed he was agreeing to my request. As I dug his harness out from under the checkout counter, he leapt up on top of the counter, waiting for me to slip it on him. A few moments later I had pulled the vest-like garment over Rattlesnatches head and had snapped and tightened the straps that held it on him. Next, I attached the leash to the metal rung that was sew into the vest between his shoulder blades, and we were ready.

Moments later, the two of us were slinking out of Head Rock Harbor Books, hoping to see no one on our journey. Typically, we didn't go on many walks. Citizens of Head Rock Harbor *loved* seeing Rattlesnatches outdoors in his harness even more than they loved seeing him in the store. So, our walks could easily turn into *stands* as people fawned over him, asked questions, and kept us from enjoying a leisurely stroll. It made me feel like the whole exercise had been pointless and Rattlesnatches was visibly annoyed by the time we got back to the store.

However, if the two of us set out during lunch time on a weekday, we could usually slip away from Harbor Street before anyone noticed. Fortunately, that was the case when we snuck out of the bookstore. Rattlesnatches led the way, slinking stealthily down the sidewalk, leading us to the corner. Before I knew it, we had rounded the corner and were on our way towards the bluff.

It was a breezy day, but the wind didn't carry the chill it had the last few days. With the sun out, it was actually pleasant—which was a good thing, since I'd forgotten to grab a jacket. Rattlesnatches had been on enough walks that he knew the route to lead us along. He never got too far ahead, pulling at his leash, though sometimes he liked to climb. If a particular tree or wall seemed especially fascinating, sometimes I'd have to coax him down.

On this particular day, Rattlesnatches seemed to be content to simply follow our route, his little paws carrying him gracefully along as he pranced. The wind whipped over his lithe little body and he held his head back regally, his ears twitching with the air. By the time we'd reached Bluff Road, Rattlesnatches was walking at a pace that forced me into longer strides to keep up.

Though I'd had no intention of walking up the hillside, since I'd been more in the mood for a leisurely stroll, I decided to let Rattlesnatches keep leading. Since most of our walks were ruined, and we hadn't had a successful long walk in a while, I wasn't going to ruin his good time. Even if it meant huffing and puffing for breath as we walked the inclines of the bluff.

I'd mentally prepared myself for the first hill when Rattlesnatches began sniffing along the curb. A slight jerk on his leash and he was prancing up the hill, carrying on as usual. He'd stop and sniff the curb here and there, as if looking for something—*probably a place to do some business*—before we'd carry on further up the hill. Trees lined either side of the road leading up the hill. In fact, every turn of the road took a person through tunnels of trees. It was the perfect place for an indoor cat to play king of the jungle and mark their territory.

I didn't particularly enjoy the thought of standing there, watching Rattlesnatches go to the bathroom. Cleaning his box twice a day at home was enough. However, he had so few chances to get out in nature and act like a wild pussycat that I decided to go with the flow. I'd had to endure worse things in my lifetime.

Fortunately, as we climbed the first hill and turned the sharp curve to the next hill that took us further up the bluff, Rattlesnatches' sniffs didn't turn into a restroom break. Surprisingly, I wasn't breathing too heavily by the time we'd made our way halfway up the second hill. Apparently, all of the trips up and down the stairs at the shop, lifting and lugging boxes of books, and walking everywhere in town had put me in better shape than I'd known.

By the time we were cresting the top of the second hill, I was feeling mighty proud of myself, ready to conquer the third hill. Of course, much further up and we'd start passing the houses of people who lived on the bluff, and we'd be forced to turn around. People up on the bluff didn't like the townies using *their* roads for leisure activities—like walking an adorable cat in a harness. Rich people are often joyless, I've found.

Rattlesnatches must have remembered how far up on the bluff we were allowed to venture, because at the crest of the second hill, he found interest in the curb again. He didn't sniff and prance away as he had all the other spots on our way up; his nose was more than mildly interested in the spot. *Finally,* I had thought to myself, *he'll do his business and we'll be done with that.*

When Rattlesnatches sniffed at the curb again, jerked back, and then looked up at me, his eyes wide with excitement, I frowned. There was nothing on the curb. No bugs or litter or anything all that fascinating. Certainly nothing to make him leap with surprise.

"Just do your business," I said out of the corner of my mouth, "and we can move on like it never happened. I didn't see it, okay?"

Rattlesnatches mewled up at me.

Frowning, I looked down at him, wondering what had gotten him to alert in such a way. I stepped up on the curb, still holding his leash and inspected the grassy strip. Nothing was to be found on the curb or the grassy strip of land that came before the hill sloped down sharply into the trees below.

"What's the problem?" I asked, looking down at him. "I'm no cat, but it seems like a nicer place to squat than a box full of sand."

He mewled up at me again. My frown deepened, as did the crease between my brows. So, I turned and looked around some more, wondering what Rattlesnatches was bothered by so deeply. The wind off the river ruffled my hair, and it was a bit chillier up on the second hill than down in town, but nothing seemed odd. The slope down to the trees below was vertiginous, but Rattlesnatches was unlikely to slip and slide down the hill. The strip of grass was large enough for me to keep my footing easily. For a cat, it was practically a playground.

"What in the world has gotten you so confused?" I asked, turning and looking around.

A gust of wind whipped up the hillside and slapped me in the face, nearly throwing me off balance. I chuckled to myself and stepped back from the crest of the hill. Rattlesnatches mewled again. A flash of silver caught my eye below, and I turned as the wind ruffled the freshly leafed trees below.

That was when I noticed the slight impression of tire tracks in the grass down the hillside that led into the trees. If we hadn't stopped and looked around so thoroughly, I never would have noticed the tracks leading down the hill into the wooded area. And I wouldn't have seen the silver Toyota buried in the trees at the base of the hill.

CHAPTER TEN

"Well," Marv stepped out of the trees and walked across the grassy patch towards me, "that's just an unfortunate situation."

"Is it Marshelle's car?" I asked.

Chief Bucksworth and Officer Ashley Riley had responded when I'd called into the police department from my cell phone. Not wanting to mess with anything, Rattlesnatches and I had ventured back down the hill to stand on the roadside by the trees so they'd know where we'd found the car. In a small town like Head Rock Harbor, Marv and Ashley had made it to us in under five minutes. Rattlesnatches and I stood back as they got out of the cruiser and ventured into the trees.

The wooded area was thick enough that I couldn't see the silver Toyota from my spot on the road, even though I had been able to see a flash of it from above. However, I had only seen one silver Toyota out by the bluff in the last few days, so Marshelle was my first guess. Why she would abandon her car in the woods on the bluff was beyond me, though.

"I'm guessing so," Marv said, fluttering his hands against the thighs of his pants to clean them as best he could. "Looks like hers anyway."

"You knew Marshelle?" I asked. "I just met her yesterday for the first time."

"Been up to the place a handful of times," Marv said as he reached up to scratch his chin, then he leaned in to speak quietly, as if we weren't alone. "Ole Prescott had a few...*flights of fancy*...from time to time. Catch my drift? Thought people were after him."

Marv fluttered his fingers by the side of his head.

"Man was harmless, but he was sick, you know?" Marv continued, bending over to give Rattlesnatches a quick stroke. "Marshelle would call me up there to calm him down a bit. Give him reassurance that he was safe. So, I got to meet both of 'em a handful of times."

"Oh."

"Nice enough gal," Marv said. "Quiet. Same as Prescott. Liked to keep to themselves, I suppose."

"Yeah," I said. "She mentioned something about that."

"Gonna go over to the car and run the tag, but I'm pretty sure that's her car," Marv said. "Riley's rifling through the glovebox now, trying to find some insurance or registration, but it was full of crap."

"Okay," I said as Marv stepped past me to head towards his car. "Marv?"

"Yeah?" He turned to look at me.

"It seemed like—from the tracks in the grass down the hill—that she went over the second hill and down into the trees," I said.

"Seems that way. Must have been going at a decent pace. Got buried in there good. Made both the hood and the trunk pop. Cracked the windshield pretty nicely. Big spiderweb, actually."

"Well," I frowned, "why would she just leave the car there? Surely, she would have called y'all over at the station to let you know about the wreck?"

Marv chuckled with a shrug.

"People do weird things, Jackson," he said. "Maybe she'd had a nip or two and didn't want a ticket or to get arrested? Maybe she was driving like a wild woman and thought we'd ticket her? Who knows what gets into people's heads after accidents. They're more worried about the trouble they might get into as opposed to the trouble they're already in."

Laughing nervously, I nodded.

"I guess so," I said. "But a wreck like that? She just walked away?"

Marv thought about that and nodded. "I'll get Gloria to call the local clinics and the hospital. See if Marshelle checked in for treatment."

"Good idea," I said. "Thank her for dispatching y'all over here so quick, would you?"

"Will do," Marv said and headed towards his car.

He made his way over to his car to call Gloria, the day dispatcher, and Rattlesnatches and I went back to staring at the trees. The wind had picked up slightly, blowing off the river and over that first hill we were stood upon. Racking my brain for reasons, I couldn't quite figure out why anyone wouldn't report a wreck like Marshelle's. Surely, she'd at least need to report it to her insurance? If she had insurance. I could only assume that she did.

At the very least, Marshelle should have reported the accident simply so she could get a tow truck out to pull her car out of the trees. There'd be no way to get the damages looked at, paid for, and fixed if it stayed in the trees forever. A thought began chewing at the corner of my mind.

"Marv?" I hollered over my shoulder towards his car. "Was Marshelle's stuff in the trunk still?"

"*Nah! Empty!*" he hollered back before mumbling something into his radio.

A deep frown settled on my mouth and the furrow between my brows became a canyon. If a woman has a car accident so severe, there had to be some physical proof she had been in an accident. A bloody forehead. A limp. If Marshelle had gotten hurt in an accident—and I was certain she had since it would be miraculous not to—and then grabbed her things out of the trunk…where did she go?

I began walking towards the trees as I thought. Rattlesnatches pranced ahead of me, seemingly picking up on my thoughts.

If Marshelle had marched into town, bleeding, limping, carrying suitcases or boxes, someone would have noticed. As much as people gossiped in town over the smallest thing, a bloody lady stumbling down from the bluff carrying a suitcase would be a hot topic. No one had so much as whispered about seeing Marshelle—and the bookstore was a hotbed for the beginning rumblings of gossip. In fact, no one ever mentioned Marshelle in the bookstore—even before Prescott had died.

Rattlesnatches and I picked our way over the brush as we ventured through the trees towards the car. Our journey wasn't far—the trees and brush were just dense enough to easily conceal the car from the road. Officer Riley gave me a smile and a nod when Rattlesnatches and I appeared, then went back to picking through the car. He was still sorting through Marshelle's belongings in the glovebox.

With the trunk pointing in my direction and the hood of the car facing the other way, I immediately saw that Marv hadn't been lying. All of Marshelle's belongings had been removed from the trunk. Frowning, I stepped up and gazed inside to find that not so much as a tire iron or a toolbox. The trunk was completely empty.

Rounding the car, with Rattlesnatches at my heels, I gazed through the driver's side backseat window. A few pieces of trash in the floorboard, typical signs of the car having once had an owner. I moved up to the open driver's door and bent down to look inside.

The windshield was one big spiderweb, as Marv had said. I didn't spot any signs of blood from Marshelle hitting her head or injuring herself in any way, but the steering wheel was turned so that the Toyota logo was upside down. I popped my head out of car to look at the front wheel over the door. The wheel was turned completely to the left, which was odd. The tire tracks in the grass had been straight down the hill. With the tires turned, the car should have gone down the hill at an angle and the tracks should have been indicative of it.

Furthermore, I thought to myself, the hood of the car was facing the hill it had come down. That meant the car had come down the hill backwards. With the angle of the tires, and the backward movement, the car's rear would probably be pointing to the left. However, the car was positioned in such a way that it seemed to come straight down the hill, lose momentum in the trees, and simply stopped, coming to a gentle rest.

So...why was the steering wheel and the wheels turned?

I looked down at Rattlesnatches. I didn't know if he could read my mind, but the steering wheel and the wheels bolstered the theory brewing in my head.

Someone had used the steering wheel as a brace to pry themselves out of the car after a traumatic wreck. Probably one that had slammed their head into the windshield, causing it to spiderweb. Holding onto the wheel and pushing out of the car might have turned the steering wheel sharply, and of course, the wheels.

The person who did had pried themselves out of the car was obviously Marshelle Martin. So, it stood to reason that she had gotten out of the car, taken her things out of the trunk and walked away from the wreck. However, as I had surmised earlier, she had to have looked a hot mess. After hitting her head on the windshield, she had to have been bloody and bruised. Disoriented. She would have drawn attention to herself when she made it into town.

But no one had mentioned seeing a woman limping through town looking a mess.

When Rattlesnatches and I made eye contact again, I was certain we both had the same thought. I pushed away from the car and turned to look around the wooded area. After a traumatic head injury from a car wreck, a person wouldn't systematically go to the trunk of their car, grab their things, and waltz in a straight line back to town. They would probably take a second to figure out which direction they needed to walk. The wooded area was small, so no matter which direction Marshelle had walked, she would have exited the trees within a minute or two, even with a limp and carrying personal belongings.

However, there was no guarantee that she had taken the most direct path, which would have been walking a straight line away from the trunk to the road. I'd have to suggest to Marv that the wooded area should be searched for any signs of Marshelle dropping personal belongings as she made her path away from the car. At least that would tell them which way she walked when she left the scene. Before I could think to mention it to Officer Riley, Rattlesnatches was pulling at his leash.

"*Meow.*"

Rattlesnatches looked over his shoulder at me as he pulled at the leash, trying to venture off further into the woods. He was trying to pull me directly from my spot by the car door in a straight line away from it. With nothing better to do, I indulged him. Rattlesnatches began prancing as I began to walk, giving him slack on the leash.

Stepping over branches and sticks, piles of leaves, and other detritus, I followed Rattlesnatches through the woods about ten yards. Finally, he stopped ahead of me and sat back on his haunches. He looked over his shoulder at me, his eyes opening and closing languidly as he waited for me to catch up. When I finally approached, I didn't have to think long about why he had been urging me to follow him.

Rattlesnatches had stopped at the lip of a gully that ran through the wooded area. Obviously, there was no way he could have gone further into the woods without sliding down the gully. I laughed to myself as I bent down to scratch his ears.

"Sorry, little guy," I said, kneeling beside him. "Your path has come to an—"

I didn't have time to finish my statement. A flutter of fabric at the bottom of the gully caught my eye and I whipped my head over to see what the breeze had kicked up.

Marshelle Martin was laid out in the gully. Face down. Her head a bloody mess.

She didn't have any belongings with her.

Not that she would ever need them again.

CHAPTER ELEVEN

The lunch rush was over, most of the afternoon had come and gone, and the dining room of Munchies was essentially empty. So, Lardell and Shirley were pretending to visit with each other over by the passthrough to the kitchen. Of course, they were actually watching Marv interrogate Charlene and me, but we were all too polite to mention it. Interrogate was kind of a strong word, anyway. Marv was simply getting information from Charlene and I about Marshelle since we were, apparently, the last two people to see her alive. That was an assumption since no one seemed to know where Marshelle went after she left the Pemberton place on Sunday.

Marshelle wrecking out after leaving the Pemberton home and being left there for 2 days was somehow sadder than the wreck and her death on their own. No one should take that long to be found when they die. There had been no one to say she hadn't shown up where she was expected. No one expecting her to show up at a certain time at some place so they would know to call and check on her, actually.

Marshelle Martin had driven down the bluff, had a wreck, died, and if I hadn't taken Rattlesnatches for a walk, I'm not certain anyone would have known she was missing. From what I'd gathered from Marv in the half hour the three of us had been talking, he'd yet to locate a family member or friend to reach out to about her death. Of course, it was only a matter of time before Marv found *someone* who would have some interest in her passing, but the time it was taking was depressing.

"So, let me get this straight," Marv said, reaching up to pinch the bridge of his nose. "She gave y'all the spare key I asked her to drop off...and left?"

Charlene nodded vigorously.

"Yeah," I said. "She barely even came into the house. She said she'd packed up her personal belongings, cleaned the fridge out of perishables, and gave us the key."

"She didn't say anything else?" he asked.

I shrugged. "I briefly gave my condolences about Prescott and she mentioned how sad it was. She thanked me for helping and told me to thank Charlene, and then she left."

"Thank Charlene?" he asked. "Why didn't she thank Charlene herself?"

He glanced over at Charlene—who he had called to meet us at Munchies once him and Officer Riley had the wreck scene secure—and she flinched.

"I'd gone off looking around the house," Charlene said. "Jackson stayed talking to her while I wandered off."

"Ah," Marv said.

"And if I'd known then what I know now, I wouldn't have let her leave," Charlene grumbled.

I turned my head to look at her, confused.

"What's that now?" Marv asked.

"Well, Jackson will back me up here," Charlene said, nodding at me confidently. "All of Prescott's artwork is missing. That Marshelle said she already packed up her stuff. She probably took it all with her."

"Hold on," I said. "You're assuming there was art to take from the house, Charlene. Marv, we have no reason to think—"

"I'd put money on it, Jackson," Charlene whisper-hissed, shooting a glance at Lardell and Shirley. "Not a single bit of finished artwork in that studio? She beat us to it! She got to it before we could!"

"Whoa," I said, holding my hands up defensively. "I'm not trying to get Prescott's artwork."

"You know what I mean," Charlene snipped. "Without artwork an auction will be worthless. And I find it impossible to believe that Prescott Pemberton didn't have a single painting finished in his studio. That woman must have—"

"Okay," Marv said, indicating that everyone needed to quiet down. "Okay. Okay. We're talking about the dead here, Charlene. Let's have some decorum."

Charlene huffed, crossed her arms over her chest, and sunk back in the booth seat. I shifted next to her, as though I could put more distance between us. Marv stared at us from across the table.

"Charlene didn't have anything with her anyway," I said, finally. "There was no artwork in that car. If she had the wreck right after she left—"

"It would have been in the car, right." Marv nodded slowly. "Sorry, Charlene. I don't think Marshelle took anything. Nothing you'd care about anyway."

Frowning, I nearly let my next thought fall out of my mouth. I kept it to myself. As long as Charlene was around, I'd continue to remain tight-lipped.

"Then where are all the paintings?" Charlene threw her hands up.

"Maybe he never got over his artist's block…or whatever?" I suggested. "He came home from New York to let the river air…*soothe*…whatever was bothering him in New York, and it didn't work. He'd only been back a year. It takes time to get over things."

Marv was eyeing me.

"Marshelle said he was having a few small medical issues in New York," I explained quietly. "And, apparently, he had been on the wagon until the night he died. He was dealing with a lot. Maybe his art had taken a backseat to all of his personal problems?"

Charlene huffed again. Marv shook his head at her and looked down at his notepad.

"So," Marv sighed, "to wrap this all up. She wasn't acting funny. She didn't say anything funny. All seemed normal?"

"It was the first time I met her, but she seemed okay," I said.

Charlene begrudgingly nodded. "She seemed fine."

For a few moments, Marv flipped through his notes, jotted a few more down, and looked us both over, as though making sure we were being honest. I was fairly certain he was happy with what I had to say, but Charlene had upset him. No one could blamed Marv for being annoyed with Charlene. Worrying about a man's artwork when he and his personal assistant were dead seemed like bad taste at the least. Insensitive and uncaring, for sure.

"Well," Marv grumbled and slid from the booth seat across from us, "I suspect that's about it. I can't really imagine we'll need much else. Seems pretty straightforward, doesn't it?"

I didn't know what to think—or say—so I stared up at him. Charlene didn't bother responding either. One thought did cross my mind that I felt I could share.

"One of you might want to call Prescott's family and tell them Marshelle is dead," I said. "She seemed to know the family well enough that they might be interested to know she's gone."

"Well, I'm not doing it," Charlene pushed out of the booth and stood up defiantly at the end of the table to stare down at me. "I'm not good at giving bad news."

Then she turned on her heels and marched away from us and out of Munchies. The bell was still tinkling over the door when Marv turned to me, and I knew exactly what he was going to suggest.

"Shouldn't the law do it?" I asked before he said anything. "This is a death we're talking about."

"Would you, though?" he asked. "Just get them prepared for when I eventually have to call and talk the *business* side of things?"

"Interrogate them about their whereabouts and what the last thing she said to them was?"

"I didn't interrogate y'all none," Marv said, grinning sheepishly.

I sighed. "Get me the sister's number. I'll call her when I get back to the store."

"I appreciate your help, Jackson," Marv said. "I've gotta go over and get Morris out of bed so he can start his shift early and help us with all this mess."

Marv sifted through his notepad, staring down at it as he jotted a note.

"I'm sure he'll be pleased," I said.

"Here," Marv said, handing me a ripped-out piece of notepad paper. "That's the sister's number. Give me a holler once you've talked to her. Her names Rita Johnson. Married and widowed."

"Will do," I said, taking the paper and slipping it into my pocket. "I've gotta get back to Rattlesnatches anyway. Taking him to the shop and then coming here to talk to you probably confused the heck out of him."

Marv chuckled and began to walk away.

"Marv?" I asked, stopping him.

"What's up?" He turned back to look at me.

"There wasn't any artwork in Marshelle's car."

"That's a fact," he said. "She didn't take nothing she shouldn't have. Charlene's crazy."

Nodding, I said, "There weren't any boxes or bags of her own things in the car, either."

It took a moment, but Marv finally caught my drift. His shoulders slumped and his face went blank, as though this information had reset him.

"If Marshelle had cleaned out her stuff that morning, came to see you, and you sent her right back up to give us the key, her stuff still should have been in the car," I said. "Unless she was storing it all somewhere else. But I don't think that's likely. She lived at Prescott's and she made it sound as though she was heading out for New York as soon as she left. So…it's unlikely she dropped her things off somewhere else."

"Sounds right."

"So…where *are* her things?" I asked.

Marv stood there for a moment, then gave me a lopsided grin.

"I guess that's one of the things we'll be looking into, Jackson."

Then he gave me a sharp nod and headed out of Munchies. I'd obviously gotten under the chief's skin with my question. I often get under a lot of people's skin with all of my questions. Usually because I ask questions they should have thought of without my help. People, but cops especially, usually aren't happy when you point out that they missed something that was right in front of their faces.

By the time I'd climbed out of the booth, said goodbye to Shirley and Lardell, and walked back down to the bookstore, my head was spinning with thoughts. More questions were pinging off the spaces between my ears than I could keep up with at the moment. And I was beginning to get a sick feeling in my stomach about the two unfortunate, unexpected deaths that had happened in our small town over the course of a week.

Rattlesnatches was waiting in the chair outside of the apartment door upstairs, lazily curled up, drifting off to sleep, when I returned to the shop. My intention had been to go upstairs and call Prescott Pemberton's sister from my cell phone. However, when I looked down at Rattlesnatches, comfy and cozy in the chair, I had a thought. I didn't want strangers to have my personal phone number. Then they could bother me when I was trying to be lazy.

I marched back downstairs to the check-out counter and picked up the store's phone. Pulling the slip of paper Marv had given me out of my pocket, I quickly dialed the number for Prescott's sister. Not getting an answer on the other end had been my hope. However, after a few rings, the call was answered, and I did my best to welcome the interaction.

"*Hello?*" A woman's voice sounded from the other end of the line.

"Hello," I said. "Is this Rita Johnson? This is Jackson Harper. From Head Rock Harbor? I'm trying to reach—"

"*Oh, yes!*" the woman said. "*Charlene's assistant!*"

I paused for a moment, my eyes closing slowly as I swallowed the knee jerk response that boiled up in my throat. After a moment, and a deep breath, I resumed the conversation.

"I own Head Rock Harbor Books," I said calmly. "Charlene had asked me to help her assess your family home and contents for an auction?"

"*Yes, yes!*" she said. "*It's so kind of the two of you to help us out like this. I don't know when I would even be able to get out to Head Rock Harbor to handle this all myself. You don't know how much my mother and I appreciate this.*"

Though Rita sounded happy to have us helping her, there was an underlying sadness to her voice. Of course, with her deceased brother being the reason for her needing our help, that was understandable. The way things sounded, her caring for her elderly mother and all, there were probably also other factors that made her sound less than thrilled with life.

"We're happy to help, Ms. Johnson," I said. "Unfortunately, I—"

"Do you think an auction is even worthwhile? I don't know if—"

I took my turn cutting her off.

"Ms. Johnson," I began, "I'm not calling about the auction today. I'm sorry to break this to you—but our Chief of Police asked me to reach out to you."

"Oh?" Concern filled her voice.

"This afternoon, just after lunch," I said, "I was walking and found Marshelle Martin's car had been involved in a wreck. Not far from the house? Well…she didn't survive the crash."

There was a long pause, and I nearly began speaking again to fill the silence, but Rita finally cleared her throat.

"I'm not sure I know who that is, dear," she said.

Confused, my brow furrowed. "Marshelle Martin? Prescott's assistant? She was living at the house with him?"

"I see!" Rita responded. *"I wasn't aware he'd had an assistant. I'm glad to know he wasn't alone out there, though. My brother could certainly seclude himself from the world if you let him. I'm glad he didn't do that."*

Frowning, and more confused than ever, I started to speak, but Rita beat me to it.

"I'm sorry to hear about her death, though," Rita said. *"That's so unfortunate. Does she have any family we can reach out to?"*

"Well," I said, collecting my thoughts quickly, "Chief Bucksworth is working on that. We just found her today, so everything is…fresh. But I'm sure if he finds out who you can send your condolences to, he'll let you know."

"Wonderful. Please let him know that I appreciate all he's doing."

"I will," I said. "Ms. Johnson—"

"*Oh, just call me Rita!*" she said happily. "*Ms. Johnson is so formal for someone doing such a nice thing for our family.*"

"Sure. Rita. Um, another thing I might want to mention—while we have the chance to speak—I'm not sure that there is a lot in the house that will bring much money at an auction. Maybe some of the furniture and appliances? The house itself is probably what will be worth selling. Have you ever thought about doing an as-is sale—house and all contents? I know this is a lot to think about right now—I'm asking a lot of you while you're still grieving—but while I have you on the phone…"

"*Of course,*" Rita said. "*I understand. There really isn't anything exciting in the house, I can agree with that. We never were the kind to have antiques or anything incredibly fancy. An as-is sale might be best.*"

"I'll keep that in mind as we finish up figuring out what to do," I said. "And I'll let Charlene know."

"*Wonderful. I just ask that you set aside Prescott's paintings. We'll want those crated and shipped to us, of course.*"

My frown deepened to such a degree I thought my face would split.

"Ms. Johns—Rita?" I began. "I'm surprised Charlene hasn't spoken to you yet, but we haven't found any paintings that Prescott finished. All that was in his studio was one he had started. And it had *barely* been started. We haven't found any completed paintings to crate and ship to you."

"*Oh. Oh, no. I…well, I don't know what to say. Prescott had been so optimistic every time we spoke on the phone. He*" *said the river air was doing him good. He even said he had an idea for a series of paintings.* The twelve seasons of the Midwest. *I think he was going to make a painting to represent each month on the river there in Head Rock Harbor. He said he was so focused that some nights he slept in his studio.*"

"I'm so sorry to have to deliver that news," I said. "We didn't find any paintings, let along twelve depicting seasons here."

I really was sorry. Charlene should have been the one to tell the family. How I had gotten dragged into this mess was beyond me—but it was annoying the heck out of me.

"But so far…there hasn't been any artwork to bother with saving," I finished.

"*It's not your fault, dear,*" Rita said gently. "*Artists! You know? What he thought was progress could be nothing to others. Who can understand an artist's mind except another artist? I'd just hoped that after all the times he talked about all the work he was inspired to complete that we'd have at least a handful of his paintings to enjoy.*"

"I'm sorry," I said, chewing at my lip.

"*No wonder,*" Rita said. "*He'd been sober for so long. Maybe this is what did it?*"

"Uh…what do you mean?"

"*Well,*" Rita said, "*not being able to work—having so much difficulty even starting a painting—that must have been what drove him back to the bottle.*"

I thought about that. "Maybe."

Silence drew thick on the phone line.

"*Well,*" Rita said with a sigh, "*you and Charlene do the best you can and you just let me know what we're going to do. I trust you both to make the best decision about an as-is sale."*

Rita Johnson and I made our pleasantries and said our goodbyes to each other before hanging up. I sat there on the stool behind the check-out counter, more confused than ever. Even more questions than I had before were flooding my brain as I stared out at the darkening bookstore. Finally, I shot off a text to Marv, letting him know that Rita wasn't going to be too concerned about Marshelle Martin's death.

Then I grabbed my jacket and headed back out. I needed to clear my head.

CHAPTER TWELVE

In Head Rock Harbor, you really have two options when it comes to *clearing your head.* Or, at least, if you use the method I use for clearing your head, there are only two options. There's Bernie's Tavern and then there's Harper's Bar & Grill. Bernie's, while able to get the job done, is a little too rough of a crowd for me. Bernie himself is a nice enough fellow, but his patrons get rowdy after the sun goes down. I prefer my drinks don't come with a knuckle sandwich.

Typically, if I wanted to drink, I'd go to Harper's. My mom's place, while rowdy at times, never got dangerous or violent. It wasn't that the potential for rowdy townies to start swinging at each other wasn't there, it was that everyone feared Deb Harper. The biggest, burliest guys in town knew that there wasn't a man my mother feared. If you started tearing up her joint, you might end up in the river. Permanently.

Being Deb's son, I was about the only person who could give her much sass. Then again, she didn't really put up with a lot from me, either. At least not in public. That was why I didn't tell her to find a better place to sit when she plopped down on the stool beside me at the bar.

When I'd first gotten to Harper's, the bar area was still fairly vacant, seeing that the dinner rush hadn't quite gone by and the sun was still slowly sinking towards the horizon. The regular drinking hour and the time for getting rowdy was still an hour or so off. It was the perfect time for me to clear my head. However, within a minute of my arrival, and before the first drink was even pushed in front of me by Cleo, the bartender, Deb had parked herself next to me.

"You see that group of young men over there?" she asked quietly.

Or as quietly as Deb could ever manage. Anyone within six feet could have heard Deb's "whispers." Fortunately, she wasn't talking about anyone within six feet of us.

"Huh?"

"That booth full of young men." Deb flicked her head towards the dining area as she pulled her cigarette wallet out of her half-apron. "Back corner."

Cleo set a bottle of Blue Moon and a shot of Jack Daniels in front of me as I turned my head discreetly to look at the booth Deb mentioned. Across the restaurant, at the far other end in the dining area, the back corner booth was occupied by a group of four guys. Most my age or maybe a year or two younger. They all seemed to be of legal drinking age.

"Yeah?" I shrugged as I turned my attention to my drinks. "Thanks, Cleo."

Cleo St. Clair, bartender, cabaret performer, and sometimes stripper, gave me a friendly nod. Then she went back to cleaning glasses and prepping for the rush later. Her silky black shoulder length hair had been pulled up into a high ponytail. Her tight black tank top, black jeans, biker boots, and studded jewelry told customers unfamiliar with Harper's that this wasn't the place and she wasn't the one.

"That one in the corner," Deb said, striking up a Newport before stuffing her cigarette wallet back into her half-apron, "could be my son in law."

"You got a kid looking to get married?" I asked with a snort, then knocked back my shot of whiskey.

"He's gay," Deb said, ignoring me. "He didn't come right out and say it, but a mother knows these things. He is *good lookin'*."

I cast a glance at the guy discreetly again. He looked like Jeremy. I shuddered.

"We all have a type, I suppose," I said.

I tapped the shot glass as I took a swig of my beer and Cleo gave me a nod.

"I bet you he could de-crème a Twinkie without taking the wrapper off." Deb sighed.

"*Ma!*" I nearly fell off my stool.

Deb cackled and coughed on her smoke. Cleo poured me another shot as she tried not to grin. She had been pretending not to listen to us, so a grin would have blown her cover.

"Don't say stuff like that," I whisper-hissed at Deb. "Not to me, anyway."

"Oh, grow up," Deb cleared her throat and turned on her stool to face me.

I stayed sitting forward, facing the bar as I kicked back the second shot. I pushed the glass to the edge of the bar, indicating I was done with shots for the evening. Two was my limit. Beer would have to suffice for the rest of the evening. Moderation. Always moderation with alcohol.

"You haven't been on a date since I don't know when," Deb continued. "I'm looking out for my investments."

"Your...*investments?*"

"When I pushed you out, I assumed it would continue the family line. You're dragging tail, so I'm trying to light a fire under you."

Groaning, I took a sip of my beer.

"I'd like a son in law," Deb reiterated as she smoked thoughtfully. "Some grandkids one day wouldn't be a horrible idea. Make Christmas more exciting, at least."

"Deb—"

"You're pushing thirty, Jackson. No time to waste."

"*I'm twenty-seven years old.*"

"Clock's a tickin'."

"I don't have any part of me that's going to ruin my chances if I don't procreate now, Mom," I said. "And there's no rush to find a son in law. We're both young. You're forty-three for God's sake."

Deb punched me in the arm.

"You shut your smart mouth."

"Ow!" I chuckled. "What did I say?"

"You don't go 'round here talkin' about my age. Or taking the Lord's name in vain."

I laughed into my bottle and took a sip. Deb was smiling, so I knew she wasn't too upset.

"I don't think the Lord is listening in at Harper's, Deb," I said. "He knows where he isn't welcome."

Deb cackled.

"Likely, he knows a lost cause when he sees it," she said as she stubbed out her Newport. "All's I'm saying is that boy over there is mighty good to look at and you haven't looked enough lately."

"You don't know if I've been…*looking*…or not."

"Fair," Deb said and lit another cigarette. "But I know you haven't introduced me to my future son in law yet, either."

"Are people even allowed to smoke in here?" I waved a hand in front of my face. "Isn't there some ordinance?"

"Yeah. *Don't get caught.*"

The two of us laughed and I sipped at my beer as Deb smoked her cigarette in silence for a few moments. I finished the Blue Moon in record time and gestured for another from Cleo. Once she had cleared my old bottle and set a fresh one in front of me, Deb kicked at my shin with the toe of her shoe.

"So," she said, blowing smoke away from us, "what's got your britches itchy?"

"Pardon me?"

"You only come in to drink when you're bothered by something," Deb said. "So? What's got you all in your head?"

"Nothing." I waved her off.

An older couple who had finished their dinner wandered into the bar and set up camp at the pool table. The man went to the jukebox and slid some money into the slot as the woman began feeding quarters into the table. I knew my time at Harper's was drawing to a close.

"Don't worry about it," I said.

"Jackson Francis Harper," Deb began, making me cringe, "if you make me pry this out of you, you are not going to be happy."

"Cut it with the middle name stuff, Mom."

She grinned. "Then get to talkin'. The rush is about to start."

As if taking her cue, the jukebox cranked up at that moment and *I Walk the Line* by Johnny Cash began playing. Loudly.

"It's nothing, really," I said. "It's just...that thing with Prescott Pemberton?"

"The painter?" Deb leaned in to be heard over the music.

"Yeah, him," I said. "His death and—"

"That assistant of his and the car crash?" Deb asked, puffing on her cigarette.

"How'd you...oh, yeah. Head Rock Harbor."

Deb grinned at me and blew out smoke.

"Anyway," I said, "it's all just...*odd*. Right?"

"How do you mean? People die all the time. Someone's dying right now."

"You know what I mean, Deb," I said. "Prescott seemed like a typical death—unfortunate and untimely—but typical. Now with Marshelle and...things just seem odd. That's all. And I don't think Marv is finding anything all that odd about it, so I don't think he's going to be looking into it all that much. It'll all be shut and closed tomorrow, I'm sure. I'm not certain that's good."

Deb huffed out a sigh, smoke rolling out of her nostrils like a dragon as she stubbed out her cigarette. She gestured for Cleo to take away the ashtray before any other patrons got any ideas. Then she focused her attention back on me.

"Mind your business, Jackson," Deb finally said. "That's what I'd say to you. Go over there and get me a son in law and mind your business."

"Ma—"

"Ma nothin'," Deb cut me off. "This is none of your business and Marv will do his job the best he can."

"That's what I'm afraid of," I mumbled.

Deb punched me in the arm again.

"Run your bookstore, mind your business, and stay out of it," Deb said. "Harpers don't get involved in police business."

She slid from her stool.

"The ones with criminal records, sure," I said with a snort.

Deb was digging in her half-apron. "I'm going to pretend I didn't hear that sass. Here. Take this."

I looked down to find Deb holding a credit card out to me.

"What's that?" I asked, sliding it from her hand into mine.

"Germ left his credit card here last night," she said. "He was playing big spender with that new little boy toy of his. *They've been getting cozy, lately.* Anyway, I texted him and he said to give it to you because he'd probably see you soon."

"He'll probably see you first. You own the bar, after all."

She laughed. "Well, I'm just doing as requested."

"All right," I said, sliding the credit card into my pocket. "He's always leaving his stuff everywhere. He left his keys at the apartment the other night after dinner and a movie and I had to chase him down. He's always leaving them at his house and having to go back for them. I'll drop the credit card by his house on my way home. He's probably out with Marv looking at the crime...the scene."

Deb rolled her eyes and gave me a nod, and then she was gone. I finished the last third of my beer in one swallow, gave Cleo a nod and threw down enough cash to cover my tab and a decent tip, then slid from the stool. Meals at

Harper's were always free, but my mother wasn't nearly as generous with my bar tab. Since I only came in for drinks once or twice a month, it wasn't going to break me.

As I made my way from the bar and towards the front door, my eyes were drawn to the corner booth. The Jeremy doppelganger looked up in time to catch my eye. A slow, easy smile formed on his face and I forced a smile back. Before any other interaction could occur, I slipped out the front door and was on my way.

The sun had barely dipped below the horizon when I left Harper's, leaving the sky deep red, orange, violet and purple, with a velvety navy blanket overhead. Though I really hadn't drank that much at Harper's, and I wasn't quite stumbling, my walk was jaunty and a bit unique. I made it to Jeremy's house in record time.

I passed his mailbox and made my way up to the porch. Leaving his credit card in his mailbox was desperately asking someone to commit identity theft. Slipping it under his welcome mat was an equally horrible idea. Looking around, I couldn't find a safe and reasonable place to leave something so important, so I dug my keys out of my pocket and let myself into his house.

"*Jeremy?*" I popped my head into the house and hollered. "*It's Jackson!*"

When no answer came, I stepped into the house, letting the door shut behind me. Quickly, I slipped into the kitchen and laid the credit card on the counter by the coffee machine. I'd text Jeremy to let him know where his card was, but I felt he'd never miss it by the coffee pot.

I didn't want to make myself at home, but nature was calling, and the walk home was a little farther than I felt I could manage. So, I slipped down the hall to the half-bathroom to take care of business. As soon as I entered the bathroom, my nose crinkled up at the smell of rotten eggs. The smell made me want to leave, but my bladder nixed that idea. So, I quickly did my business, washed my hands, and left the bathroom.

Picking up my jaunty walk, I marched back through the living room on my way out of Jeremy's house. I was already mentally preparing dinner in my head. The alcohol had gotten to me and a feast of leftovers was calling my name. When my hip bumped into Jeremy's worn-out old La-Z-Boy recliner, I actually giggled.

I corrected my stance and made sure I hadn't knocked the recliner out of place. Jeremy loved his old navy beat-up chair. If anything happened to it, he'd kill me first and ask questions later. Once I was certain that everything was as he'd left it, I headed back to the front door. Before I could take more than a step, something on the wall caught my eye.

Turning to look at the flash of color that had drawn my attention—compromised as it was—I found myself looking at a picture. Not a picture. *A painting.* After a moment of staring at the painting on the wall, I realized I hadn't seen the painting on Jeremy's wall before. Then again, I hadn't been in his house in probably over a year. Usually, Jeremy came to my house or we hung out at Harper's or Munchies. My brow furrowed as I considered what I was looking at on the wall of my best friend's living room.

It looked a lot like the style of something Henri de Toulouse-Lautrec would have painted. I didn't take time to find out if it was a framed reproduction of a famous painting. I tore my eyes away from what I was looking at and exited

Jeremy's house. I made sure the door was locked tightly behind me.

CHAPTER THIRTEEN

For the first time in the history of Head Rock Harbor Books, I didn't open at all on Wednesday. The store should have been open until lunch, but more pressing matters occupied my mind. Even with the Spring Break crowd in town and all of those tourist dollars up for grabs, selling books was the last thing on my mind.

After leaving Jeremy's house the night before, I went back to the store, locked it up tight, turned off the lights, and retired to my apartment. I ate a quick meal of leftovers barely warmed up in the microwave, then fell into bed in my underwear. Rattlesnatches and I slept for almost twelve hours. Rattlesnatches slept easily due to all of his experience from being a cat and sleep being what they do best. Jack Daniels and Blue Moon imparted the talent of sleeping onto me. Worry had its part in the process as well.

Upon waking, bleary eyed and still full of worry, I showered and dressed. After taking care of Rattlesnatches' breakfast needs, I walked down to the police station. My intentions were not clear, even to me, when I set out to speak to Marv. However, things were simply not adding up in my head about Marshelle Martin. By extension, things with

Prescott Pemberton were seeming a little fishy, as well. Maybe I was an absolute idiot, and if Marv and his team could prove my stupidity scientifically through police procedural work, I'd let it go.

However, when I arrived at the police station, Marv and Officer Riley were busy on the phones, calling Medical Examiners, trying to reach Marshelle's family, and the like. Gloria, the day shift dispatcher was busy gossiping with Linda Wagner on the phone. Our town's mayor had a direct link to everything police related, thanks to Gloria's big mouth. Not that the mayor didn't have a right to be kept in the loop, but some of the information Gloria passed along wasn't pertinent—unless you were writing a soap opera.

So, Marv parked me at his desk as he ran around chasing down information and making phone calls. He promised that he'd get to me as quickly as he could, but the minutes were ticking by rapidly and I was no closer to having a conversation with him after an hour of sitting at his desk. When I finally looked up from playing on my phone and realized that Officer Riley and Marv had both wandered off to God knew where, I was becoming frustrated.

Gloria's voice drifted down the hall from the little dispatch office, but I found myself otherwise alone. Frowning, I wondered if coming to talk to Marv about my thoughts was even worth it. Even if my thoughts were worthwhile, no one seemed to care to hear them. The only person in town who seemed to want to hear my thoughts was Charlene—and that was only if those thoughts were that an auction at the Pemberton place would make a ton of money.

"Marv?" I hollered out.

No one answered. Gloria continued to carry on her phone conversation down the hall in the dispatch office.

"Officer Riley?" I hollered again.

Still no answer. Then I had a thought.

"Jeremy?"

Again, I was left with Gloria's distant conversation as my only answer. I was about to rise from my seat and march out of the police department, and keep all of my thoughts and speculation to myself. Deb would have been proud of me. As I started to shift in my seat, a manila folder on Marv's desk caught my attention. The scratched writing on the tab was what interested me the most.

Medical Examiner's Report – Prescott Pemberton

Glancing around the office once again, I almost called out everyone's names a second time to make sure I was alone. However, I hadn't heard any footsteps or doors opening and closing. Wherever everyone had gone off to, they were still there. So, I decided that a little nosiness wouldn't hurt anyone. I slipped my index finger under the tab of the manila folder and flipped it open. Immediately, I realized that I had no idea how to read a Medical Examiner's report. I was going to do my best, though.

I was no expert, but the report seemed short. A few pages of dictated text from the ME's findings during Prescott Pemberton's autopsy. Notes about the color and condition of skin, hair, fingernails, toenails, organs, and the like. The state of undress of Prescott was mentioned in passing. I supposed because it was odd that he had been found nude outdoors. Almost every inch of Prescott's body was described in blunt, factual detail, making me hope that I didn't need an autopsy when I died. Medical terminology, when used to describe a person's body, is never flattering.

As expected, the cause of death was listed as "fall" and "blunt force trauma" to Prescott's head. The ME had noted that Prescott's fall and subsequent knock to the noggin resulted in a gash three inches long on the calvaria, along the Sagittal suture. White paint chips were retrieved from the open wound, most likely transferred from the object he fell upon. As a painter, I wondered if Prescott didn't already have some paint in his hair, and the fall onto the rock didn't push the paint into the gash. Anything was plausible.

A "vaguely fishy" smell was detected on Prescott's body. I was already thinking about the location the body was found in before I got to the next sentence that stated that fact. If you fall and die in the harbor, you're literally sleeping with fishes. A slight rash was noted along Prescott's neck, lower chin, and mouth, which was attributed to the sandy soil in which he was found.

Nothing else seemed out of the ordinary, according to the dictated notes from the Medical Examiner. Even though a fall had resulted in a tragic death, Prescott's body was otherwise normal, no significant abnormalities were found, and no other biological reason for death was determined. The fall and the hit to the head had done the job perfectly without help.

Finally, when I flipped to the last page, I found the toxicology report. Not being a lab technician or a medical expert, I wasn't certain what every number on the chart meant. However, I understood the words "negative" and "positive." And the only line item that showed positive on Prescott Pemberton's toxicology report was acetaminophen.

Tylenol. Probably. Since Prescott didn't strike me as a generic medication kind of guy. The numbers given for normal range showed that Prescott's level of acetaminophen was a little high, but not anywhere near the toxic range. Of course, if his headaches and other problems from New York had carried over to Head Rock Harbor, it would make sense that he was regularly taking high doses of an analgesic like Tylenol. That didn't seem strange to me at all.

According to the screening done of his blood, Prescott Pemberton was not on any illicit drugs or any known prescription drugs that cause impairment. Most importantly, he was stone cold sober. No alcohol—except marginal amounts that could be attributed to testing error—was in his system. Prescott Pemberton had fallen and hit his head in the harbor while sober as a judge.

I closed the manila envelope and found my eyes were focused on something I couldn't quite see. Though Marshelle's crash had seemed odd to me—especially the condition she and her car were in after the fact—Prescott's autopsy report was giving me a lot to think about, too. Of course, I wasn't sure what I was thinking. Things weren't quite adding up, but there weren't really any dots connecting, either.

As quick as I had been to pry into the report, I closed it as quickly, and rose from my seat. Marv, Officer Riley, and Jeremy were still nowhere to be seen. Gloria was still talking down in the dispatch office, and my head was full of more questions than when I'd first entered the police department. With a sigh, I straightened the report on Marv's desk, hoping he wouldn't be able to tell I'd rifled through it, and then left his office.

Moments later, outside of the police department, I found myself heading across town towards the bluff. However, when I got to the base of the hillside, instead of heading up, I hooked a left and headed to the south side of town. Within minutes, I was standing outside Bernie's Tavern. Though I wasn't entirely certain what had led me to Bernie's, I knew that I had a question only he could answer.

Stepping up to the front door, I wondered if he'd even be open so early in the day. However, Bernie's clientele wasn't the kind to worry about the numbers on a clock when it came to drinking. In their world, it was always five o'clock somewhere. So, when I pulled on the front door handle— taking note of the plywood slapped over the hole Mavis Attberry's shotgun had left—the door swung wide. The open doorway led from a sunny, slightly chilly day into a tunnel of gloom, neon, and cigarette smoke.

I sauntered inside, letting the door slap shut behind me. Surrounded by the gloom of a dark tavern lit only by old Christmas lights, the light from a T.V. screen playing some sports game, and neon signs that had seen better days, I felt depressed immediately. A lot of people—including myself—use alcohol to wash away worries. However, doing it in a place like Bernie's made the practice seem sadder somehow.

"Well," I recognized Bernie's voice immediately somehow, "that's a face we don't see in here often. Your ma stop letting you drink at her place for free?"

A couple of drunk guys in old sweaters and flat caps at the end of the bar chuckled wryly at Bernie's joke. I turned to the bar to find the man himself standing behind it, an old white bar towel over his shoulder, his hands braced wide atop the bar, staring at me.

"She never lets me drink free," I said. "It's only food she gives me."

Bernie chuckled. "Well, Deb's no dummy. Feeding your kid is one thing, but getting' 'em liquored up is another."

"How are you, Bernie?" I asked, stepping over to the bar and pulling myself up on a stool.

"Fair to Midland," he said. "What can I get ya'? Ain't got them fancy beers like Harper's, but we've got plenty."

I couldn't help but smile at what Bernie thought passed for fancy. If it wasn't Pabst or Milwaukee's Best—*which everyone in town called 'The Beast'*—it was a *fancy beer*. The Blue Moons I had drank the night before would have absolutely scandalized the man.

"I'm not drinking," I said, waving him off. "I was just wondering if you could answer a question for me. I got curious about something."

"Yeah," he said. "She *really* blew a hole clean through the door because I cut her off. That plywood ain't there for funsies."

Frowning for a second, I wondered what Bernie was talking about, but when I realized he had probably been asked a million times about Mavis and her shotgun, I laughed.

"No," I said. "Not that. Though, I'm sorry to hear Mavis did that to your door."

"Don't say her name too loud," Bernie leaned in mischievously. "You'll summon her. She's right over there nursing a bottle."

He cocked his head towards the back of the bar. I didn't bother turning on the stool to look for Mavis. Bernie had no reason to lie about her being present. Besides, Bernie wasn't wrong about saying her name. If you mentioned Mavis, and she was nearby, she'd make herself known.

"*I can hear y'all!*" she slurred from the back of the bar.

From the sound of her voice, I could tell she was in no condition to get up and walk over to bother us. I said a silent "thank you" to the man upstairs for that blessing. Bernie and I exchanged a nervous chuckle and he went about wiping the bar with a rag that needed to be cleaned just as badly as the bar.

"I was just wondering," I said, picking up where we left off, "if you remember the night before Prescott Pemberton died?"

"Who?" Bernie frowned.

"Guy they found in the harbor? The artist guy?"

"Oh, yeah." Bernie nodded. "Yeah. I remember that night. Sure."

"Maybe it's a dumb question, but…Deb said he was at her place before, but he left completely sober. She swore on it."

"Deb don't swear for nothin'," Bernie nodded. "Good as gold, her word."

I smiled tightly.

"Did he leave here hammered?" I asked finally. "Because if he didn't drink at Harper's—"

"He didn't come in that night, Jackson," Bernie said. "We didn't know the guy around here. 'Course, I knew of him because of him being the big famous artist around town, but he never set foot in here. Especially not that night."

"Really?" I asked, frowning.

"You're not the cops, so I ain't got a reason to lie." Bernie chuckled. "Though I told Marv the same thing. That man never set foot in this place. At least, not while I was behind the bar. He must have got drunk at home if he was drinking that night. Don't think The Dock was open that night. And any other place around here serving wouldn't serve someone to the point of stumbling."

Nodding, I had to agree with Bernie. Of course, I knew from the autopsy report that Prescott had been sober when he wandered down to the harbor. However, everyone had been under the impression he had been drunk and that had been the reason for his fall. So, if no one had seen him drinking or drunk, and he hadn't drunk at home, why did he wander down to the harbor nude?

"Just an unfortunate situation," Bernie snapped me back to reality. "Poor fella."

"Yeah," I said, shaking my head clear of thoughts. "Well, thanks anyway, Bernie."

"Sure you don't want a beer?" he asked.

"Thanks anyway," I said. "I've gotta get back to the shop."

"Anytime."

I slid from my stool and gave him and the old codgers at the end of the bar a friendly nod, then headed for the front door. Before I could push open the door and make my way out of the gloom, Mavis spoke up from her dark little corner.

"*You're not...goin' to asssk me?*" she slurred.

With one hand on the door, I turned to look at her. My eyes hadn't quite adjusted to the darkness of the tavern, but I could see Mavis well enough in the inky darkness at her corner table. She'd put on ratty old jeans, a moth-eaten sweater, and a pair of mud-caked boots to wander into Bernie's. Her hair, ratty gray curtains that hung limply from her head, hung in her eyes, which she was barely able to keep open.

Bernie might have wanted people to believe he didn't serve anyone to the point of stumbling, but Mavis was definitely an exception.

"Ask you what, Mavis?" I asked.

Bernie and the men at the bar chuckled behind me.

"*'Bout that...man. The artisht who...clunked hish head.*"

Holding back a sigh, I decided to be nice to Mavis. No one else ever was, so it was time she caught a break.

"I'm sorry, Mavis," I said, speaking into the shadowy corner, "do you know anything about Prescott Pemberton?"

"*Shhhhhure do.*"

Expecting Mavis to both agree that she knew something *and* quickly provide the thing she knew was like expecting to win the lottery. Though I stood there patiently, she said nothing else. After a few moments, I gave up waiting.

"Okay. Thanks, Mavis."

I started to push the door open.

"*Ghoshts got 'em,*" Mavis said, finally. "*I sheen that ghosht chasin' him. Them white sheets flappin'. He was shcreamin' 'bout them gettin' after him, too. I tried...to help him after he...fell down. But the ghosht got 'em good.*"

"The...*ghost*...got Prescott?" I asked.

More chuckles came from behind me.

"*Yep,*" Mavis nodded in the gloom. "*Knocked 'em down and left him for dead. I tried to help, but he washn't*" *anshwerin' me. I left him to shleep it off with the fishes. Didn't know he wash dead...but no one asssks me nothin'."*

I stared at Mavis for what seemed like the longest time as Bernie and the old men at the bar had a good chuckle at her expense. Finally, when it became clear that she had said all she needed to say, I gave her a gentle smile.

"Thanks, Mavis," I said. "I'll keep that in mind."

"S'no big deal."

Then I was pushing my way out into the daylight, happy to be out of the gloom and sadness that permeated Bernie's Tavern. Walking back towards Harbor Street, I bent my head to sniff at my sweater. All of the cigarette smoke in the tavern had already soaked into the material. I'd have to throw the sweater in the washer as soon as I got home.

I made a mental note to run a load of washing. The smoke was just an excuse. I'd been needing to wash a few things for a couple of days, and a Wednesday afternoon when the shop wasn't open was as good a time as any. Rattlesnatches and I could kick back and relax while the washer ran, I could read or watch T.V., and I could push all thoughts of Prescott Pemberton out of my mind.

Mavis Attberry's revelation about a ghost being the cause of Prescott's death was the final nail in the coffin for me. Not to be grim. However, the Medical Examiner's report had been clear. Prescott had fallen, knocked his noggin, and died. Obviously, that meant everything was normal—or as normal as death could be. Marshelle Martin and her wreck had nothing to do with the matter. Both incidents were coincidental, but not connected. There was nothing unusual—just tragic—about the deaths of Prescott and Marshelle.

Mavis had seen ghosts chasing after Prescott that night. And I was trying to do the same thing. I was looking for ghosts where there were none.

CHAPTER FOURTEEN

Discovering I had more than one load of washing to be done on my day off since my bedding hadn't been cleaned in two weeks, I decided to make an afternoon of it. My bedding hadn't seen any wild times for a while, unless snacking in bed counted, but it still need washing. I'd thrown my sheets and blanket into the washer and set it for a heavy cycle. Since I'd be sitting around waiting for hours while laundry washed and dried, I retrieved my basket of embroidery skeins, set up a six-inch embroidery hoop with fourteen-count Aida cloth, and started a new cross-stitch.

Recently, I'd come across a pattern online that demanded *"Don't Let the Cat Out or the Cops In."* Surrounded by several pretty flowers and a few cats, I thought it would be a perfect piece to hang just inside the door of the shop. My patrons would get a chuckle out of the piece, anyway. Whenever Marv or Jeremy stopped by, it would annoy them, so that was a bonus.

As I sat in the chair by the door into my apartment, making my little Xs on the cloth, Rattlesnatches curled up around my neck and fell asleep. I'd barely made the "D" in the saying on the cross-stitch when Rattlesnatches sat up on my shoulder, leaned down and sniffed me, then made a haughty face, and leapt down from my shoulders. He sauntered away, his tail straight up in the air, his little butt waving goodbye.

Frowning to myself, I mindlessly made a few more stitches in the cloth before my fingers stopped of their own accord. I found myself staring down, though unfocused, at the needle protruding through the cloth from the back, ready to be grabbed and pulled through. As if coming out of a trance, I grabbed the needle with my other hand and pulled it through the Aida, the shiny black thread zipping through the hole.

I pulled the thread taut and stabbed the needle into the cloth overhand on the side of the embroidery hoop. Leaning over the arm of the chair to set the hoop in the basket of embroidery skeins, I then retrieved my cell phone from my pocket. As I was searching through my contacts, I used my free hand to pull the neck of my sweater up to sniff it.

The cigarette smoke smell made me turn up my nose. Sitting there, working on my cross-stitch, the stench my sweater had picked up from being inside Bernie's Tavern for mere minutes was still present. I'd simply gotten used to smelling it, so I'd begun to ignore the smell. Probably, when I took the sweater off to wash it, I'd have noticed the smell again, but my olfactory senses had made it part of the background while I was distracted by cross-stitch.

Finding the contact I wasn't certain I actually had, I shot off a text.

Then I sat there, my toes tapping against the wood beneath my feet as I waited for a response. Sawyer Robison seemed like a pretty popular guy, so I wasn't going to be shocked if he didn't respond. However, he was the local handyman and all-around odd job guy to call in Head Rock Harbor. Without having an actual expert to present the question in my head to, Sawyer was my next best bet.

"Meow." I looked up to find Rattlesnatches standing by the top of the stairs, staring at me.

"I know, I know," I said, sniffing my sweater again. "I'm going to wash it."

"Meow."

Then he laid down with his four legs tucked under him and stared at me. Obviously, my cat was not a fan of cigarette smoke, especially how it mixed with wool. As I was beginning to wonder why the smoke from Bernie's Tavern was more noxious than that I'd encountered from Deb's cigarettes the night before, my phone dinged. Quickly, I clicked on the banner of the response text to open my phone.

It could be anything. I can meet you there in ten minutes if that works?

Smiling, I shot off a response to Sawyer that ten minutes was perfect.

Rattlesnatches watched me, fascinated, as I stripped off my sweater, leaving my t-shirt I had on underneath, and dashed into my apartment to put the bedding from the washer into the dryer. I was about to throw my sweater into the washer when I realized it was wool and would need a cold, gentle cycle. Grumbling, I threw my other dirty clothes into the washer and started a regular load. The sweater would have to be my third, final, unplanned load of the day when I got back home.

As I dashed from my apartment, keys and wallet in hand, I snatched my light jacket off of the coat hook. I was pulling it on as I stepped over Rattlesnatches at the top of the stairs, making my way down.

Moments later, I was out the front door of the shop, locking it, and stepping over to the business next door. Hoping that I hadn't gotten ahead of myself, I stepped into Charlene's Chocolates. A quick scan of the place and I found her behind the counter, rearranging a display of chocolate covered strawberries. Breathing a sigh of relief and fully entering the shop, I let the door close behind me.

"Charlene," I called out, "do you still have the two keys to the Pemberton house?"

Charlene looked up, startled, obviously not having heard me enter the shop. When she saw me, her shock turned to delighted surprise.

"Well," she said slowly, "I do. Why?"

Thinking quickly, I formulated a plausible explanation for why I needed to get into the Pemberton house without her following along.

"I know you're busy," I began slowly as I sauntered over to the counter, "but I just had an idea about the furniture in the upstairs bedroom. I was browsing the internet and I think I might have found similar antique furniture on an auction site. If it's the same brand and year, it could bring in a pretty penny at the auction."

Charlene's eyes were lighting up before I was halfway through my sentence. As the last few words were exiting my mouth, she was dashing off to the back of the shop. When she returned, her purse was cradled in her arms and she was digging for something. Obviously, she kept the keys to the Pemberton house with her at all times.

"Here they are!" she exclaimed. "Are you sure you don't need me to come with you? I can close the shop up for a few minutes. Or we could go when—"

I waved her off quickly.

"Don't worry," I said. "This should take thirty seconds once I get up there. I don't want you shutting down the shop and taking time out of your day. If I'm wrong, you'll have wasted time *and* money."

Charlene chuckled. "Well, I appreciate that. If you need any help, though…"

I tapped my pocket.

"I've got my phone. If I discover something important, I'll shoot you a text immediately."

"Text me right away either way," Charlene suggested. "I'll be dying to know what you find out!"

With that, I took one of the spare keys from her, gave her a smile and a nod, and dashed back out of the store. Knowing that I had to get to the Pemberton place quickly, I contemplated getting my car from the back of the store and driving up. However, as I was walking away from Charlene's, I saw Sawyer's pickup truck coming down Harbor Street towards me, preparing to turn at the corner towards the bluff.

I dashed down the street, waving my arms over my head, hoping that Sawyer was paying attention. Fortunately, he wasn't distracted, and stopped at the corner, waiting for me to approach. When I got to the corner, I dashed around to the passenger side as he buzzed the window down.

"Mind giving me a lift?" I asked, slightly out of breath.

"Hop on in," Sawyer said, smiling.

"Thanks," I said, popping the door and jumping up into the cab. "If we were about to race up the bluff, you would have beat me by several minutes. Unless I got my car."

I closed the door and buckled myself in quickly as Sawyer chuckled.

"I definitely would have won," he said. "And you don't trust me drive up the bluff?"

He nodded at the seatbelt.

"I'm a safety guy," I said with a shrug.

Sawyer found that funny, for some reason, and put the truck into gear, turning the corner and pointing us towards the bluff. The two of us made idle, friendly chit chat for the two minutes it took him to drive us up the hill to the Pemberton place. Fortunately, though Sawyer was a few years younger than me—*thus, obviously an immature child*—his driving was impeccable.

He parked parallel alongside the front stoop of the Pemberton place and we both hopped out of the pickup. I let us in the front door and immediately turned on the front entryway and hallway lights. I explained to Sawyer my concerns as we made our way up the stairs and down the hall to Prescott's studio. Sawyer listened intently, taking in the information I was giving him and considering it thoroughly. I appreciated that he actually took what I had to say seriously. He probably had a lot of practice listening and being patient from being a handyman to all of the older citizens of Head Rock Harbor.

When we finally got into the sun-drenched studio, Sawyer's nose crinkled a bit. I could tell that he immediately noticed the smell that I had described to him. Quickly, he began looking around for the source of the smell. I stood back to the side, waiting to see what he would come up with and if he had any suggestions.

"That's...unpleasant," he said.

Chuckling, I said, "It's still as strong as it was the other day we were up here."

"Hm."

Sawyer shuffled around the room for a moment before his eyes landed on the doorway leading into the half-bath. Immediately, he perked up and it was if a lightbulb went off over his head.

"Pipes," he said, vaguely.

"Uh...what?" I asked.

"It's been all over town, Jackson," he said, shaking his head. "The smell is coming from the pipes. It's hydrogen sulfide in the water."

"Huh?" I asked, then shook my head. "I haven't smelled it at my place."

"It's only the houses and business who get their supply from well water," he patiently explained to me. "You're probably getting treated river water."

"Oh," I said, a disappointed frown growing on my face. "How did...*hydrogen sulfide?*...get in the well water?"

Sawyer shrugged as if it was the most natural thing.

"Sulfur bacteria. Decay. Chemical reactions. It's usually mostly harmless. Just unpleasant," he said. "The city did extra chlorination and has been telling people to use activated charcoal filters if the problem persists."

"Well," I asked the logical question, "why does it still stink in here, though?"

"You need to run the water," Sawyer said. "These pipes probably still have backed up water from before it was treated. It's just sitting there, bacteria growing more. It'll be really gross if you don't run the water, flush the toilet, you get the idea. If you just let the water sit in the pipes, it's going to keep stinking."

"Oh."

"Yeah," he said. "I'm guessing this bathroom wasn't used much to begin with, and since Mr. Pemberton passed, it hasn't been used at all."

"I wouldn't think so." I agreed, then had a thought. "Would the water with hydrogen sulfide in it stink up clothes or any washing you did with it?"

"Oh, yeah," he said, laughing. "You'd want to rewash anything after you treated the smell, for sure."

"If you showered with the water, would it—"

"You'd smell just as bad. Skin picks up and holds the smell less than something like fabric, but yeah. It wouldn't make you smell all that clean. That rotten egg smell is not nice."

"Oh," I said. "Well...I guess it all makes sense, then."

Sawyer waved his hand in front of his face. "Makes you feel a little lightheaded, doesn't it?"

I chuckled. "Yeah. It's pretty bad. If you want to get out of here, I'll just run the water in the sink for a minute and flush the toilet."

"Good deal," he said. "Give the sink a minute or two and maybe flush two or three times?"

Nodding, I agreed. "You don't have to wait around. If you need to—"

"Nah." He waved me off. "I'll be down in the truck waiting to take you back to the shop. I don't have anything more important going on."

Sawyer headed towards the door, but stopped himself.

"You'll probably want to come back with some air freshener. That stuff that covers up bad odors," he said. "It sitting around smelling like this for so long, the room will need refreshing. Maybe come back on a day that you can spray the freshener and open the windows for a while."

"Makes sense," I said. "Thanks."

Sawyer gave me a grin and a nod and headed down to his truck to wait on me.

Disappointed that the mysterious smell in Prescott's studio—and all over town—was such an innocuous thing, I shuffled over to the bathroom and flipped on the light. If the smell in the studio was bad, the bathroom was even worse. It smelled downright fishy when I stepped into the closet sized room. Covering my nose with my hand, I turned on the hot and cold water and flushed the toilet. Standing there, waiting to flush the toilet again was unpleasant, but Charlene would never be able to sell the house if the smell persisted.

After running the water for a solid minute, and having flushed the toilet three times, I figured that would do the job. Returning with room deodorizer and opening the windows on a breezy day to air out the studio would finalize the chore. As I turned to leave the bathroom, a pile of dirty clothes, tossed haphazardly in the corner of the bathroom, caught my eye. I shook my head.

Men.

Some of us simply refused to pick up our own messes. Those of us gave the rest of our gender a bad name. Smiling to myself, I flipped off the light and dashed out of the studio, ready to get away from the smell.

I exited the Pemberton house the way I came, making sure to switch of lights on the way. Once I was satisfied that the front door was locked behind me, I hopped back up into Sawyer's pickup, ready to go home.

"You didn't see anything that would be worth auctioning off in there, did you?" I asked absentmindedly.

"I wasn't really looking," Sawyer said as he started up the pickup. "But there's a few cool features. Antique boot scraper. I think I saw an old Hoosier cabinet in the dining room. There are probably a few things that are worth a few hundred or thousand dollars."

"Hm."

"But they're all part and parcel with the house, right?" he said. "Someone would get more money selling the place 'as is.'"

Laughing, I said, "My thoughts exactly."

CHAPTER FIFTEEN

Thursday proved to be another busy tourist day in Head Rock Harbor and the bookstore itself. For the morning leading up to lunch, tourists and townies alike were popping in and out of the shop, snatching up paperbacks, buying little souvenir knick-knacks I had on display by the register, and browsing the stacks as though they'd never been in a bookstore before. Of course, considering the day and age, I found it easy to believe that some of my customers were stepping into a bookstore the first time in their lives.

Marv kept popping his head into the shop, looking around for me, then finding me at the register, popping back out. It was obvious that he wanted to talk to me, but could never find me at a time when I wasn't inundated with customers. Since I couldn't close the store down completely for a second day in a row—especially when business was booming—I did my best to ignore him. Even Rattlesnatches was unbothered.

He had taken up residence atop the True Crime bookshelf and curled up in a ball. He vacillated between lazily dozing and perching on the edge of the bookshelf, staring down at customers haughtily. At one point, I thought he'd join me at the check-out counter to get his daily strokes and pets from customers. However, Rattlesnatches proved to be in a bratty mood. It happened every once in a while, so I left him to his dour disposition and concentrated on selling books.

By the time lunch rolled around, I was practically chasing my final customer out the door so that I could finally have a moment to myself. I needed a short rest, to get off my feet, and eat a sandwich or two. I'd spent the entire morning on my feet, rushing around the shop, engaging customers, and being my most friendly self. My introversion was beginning to present itself.

Unfortunately, as I was closing the door to lock up for an hour, Marv popped up out of nowhere and grabbed the door, stopping me. He gave me an impish smile as we looked at each other through the glass. So, I stepped back and let him push the door open. Once he was inside, I swiftly locked the door. It was one thing to allow Marv to intrude on my lunch period, but I wasn't going to entertain any customers during my break.

"It's lunch time, Marv," I said, simply.

"I know, I know," he said, waving me off as he reached into his pocket. "But I thought you'd want to know this, seeing how interesting I found it."

My eyebrow rose with curiosity as Marv pulled his little notebook out of his breast pocket. If Marv had found something interesting enough to waste the whole morning trying to tell me about it, the information had to be fascinating.

He gave his notepad a glance, flipped a few pages, scanned a page, and flipped some more.

"My stomach is eating itself, Marv," I said.

He chuckled, then cleared his throat.

"Marshelle *Biggerstaff*," he said, then looked up from his notepad with a smile.

"Pardon?"

"Marshelle's legal last name was Biggerstaff. *Not* Martin."

"Oh," I said. "Was she married? Divorced?"

He began shaking his head as I spoke.

"Never was Martin," he said. "That's a stage name. I guess her real name was cumbersome or too...*Midwestern?*...for New York. She took Martin as her last name while she was back east."

"Well," I said, "that would explain why Rita Johnson didn't recognize the name. Of course, with a first name like Marshelle, you'd think she'd have put two and two together."

"Maybe," Marv said, scratching his chin. "Maybe not. Don't really know much about Marshelle's history with the Pemberton family or when she took the job as Prescott's assistant. But we know for certain her name was *never* legally Martin."

"Wait," I said, a thought striking me, "a *stage name*? Was she working on Broadway or something before? Was she an actress?"

"I never heard of her." Marv shrugged. "Couldn't have been too famous. And I haven't had time to get a full picture of what her life was like before she was Prescott's assistant. I've dug into her enough to know both her parents are dead. So, can't contact them for next of kin."

He scanned the paper again.

"Apparently, she's got a brother," he said, finally. "Robert's his name. We've been calling his place in New York to let him know she's passed but haven't gotten ahold of him yet. We need someone to identify and claim the body. Set up funeral arrangements, that kind of thing."

"Of course."

"That's about all I have on her right now," Marv said. "Personally, I can say she'd been working for Prescott for at least the last three months."

"Why do you say that?" I asked.

"The first time she called to have me come up there and calm him down," Marv began, "was just at three months ago. She was there then, so, she had to have been working with him at least that long."

He grinned, proud of himself.

"Checks out on my end," I said.

Grinning wider, he closed his notepad and slipped it into his breast pocket once again. I was glad to see the police chief was proud of his work. But we still had no idea how to find Marshelle's brother, so her body was going to stay with the coroner for Heaven knew how long.

With nothing to add to Marv's research, no matter how hard I racked my brain, I returned his smile and shrugged.

"Well," I said, "seems like you have your work cut out for you. But at least you know the path forward."

"Sure enough," Marv said, then turned to the door.

"Did Prescott's family tell you what to do with his...his body?"

"They're going to cremate," Marv said. "We're working on getting the paperwork to get his body transferred to the crematorium and then his ashes sent off to them. No sense in having a big funeral here when his sister and mother couldn't even attend."

"I suppose that makes sense," I said, unlocking and opening the door for him. "Thanks for stopping by and giving me the gossip on Marshelle."

Marv turned to me in the open doorway, one foot out of the store.

"Keep that under your toupee," he said. "You hear me?"

"Sure thing, Marv. Who would I tell anyway?"

With a final warning look, Marv ducked away. Laughing, I closed and locked the door and immediately made my way to the stairs. Rattlesnatches leapt down from his perch on the True Crime bookshelf and followed me up the stairs.

"Your bowl has had food in it all day," I said, looking down at him as we made our way upstairs. "You didn't have to wait for me.

"*Meow.*"

"Well, I appreciate the courtesy," I said, chuckling.

Before we were halfway up the stairs, knocking on the glass of the front door stopped us in our tracks. In unison, Rattlesnatches and I turned to look and see who was bothering us on our lunch break. Fully intending to see a potential customer waving erratically, looking to be let in to browse, I was surprised to see Jeremy at the door. Grinning goofily, he was waving at me and pointing down at the doorhandle.

Gesturing that he should let himself in, Jeremy rolled his eyes and pointed at the doorhandle again before holding his hands up passively. He said something loudly, but I couldn't quite make out what he was saying. Of course, my context clues told me that he didn't have his key with him, so I marched back down the stairs to the door. Rattlesnatches continued his journey up to his food bowl in the apartment.

"Is every police officer in this town trying to starve me?" I huffed once the door was open.

Jeremy slipped inside and I closed the door behind him. "Huh?"

"Marv was here literally a minute ago," I said. "A guy is trying to eat some lunch around here."

"Don't let me stop you," Jeremy laughed. "In fact, you got extra for your hungry best friend?"

"Where are your keys?" I demanded.

"Forgot them at home," he said, nudging me towards the stairs. "I'll grab them when I get ready to go in for shift."

"Did you find your credit card?" I asked.

Blushing, Jeremy nodded. "Thanks, Jacks. I guess I had too many drinks, and—"

"Well, Deb was looking out for you," I said, waving him off.

Jeremy nudged me towards the stairs again.

"Come on, Jacks," he said. "Hook a fella up for lunch. I'm *starving*. I haven't eaten since last night. I was busy *entertaining* this morning."

"Jeez," I said, but couldn't keep from chuckling. "Why am I tasked with filling your belly? Munchies is right down the street, and—"

"Because you have the best home cooked meals in town," Jeremy said. "One day I'll have to make an honest man out of you so I can eat your food whenever I want!"

I rolled my eyes. "You do that anyway."

We both turned and headed towards the stairs as Jeremy chuckled at me.

"I'm just heating up leftovers. Hey," I said, "run the water in your sink for a few minutes and flush the toilet in your half bathroom a few times."

"Huh?" Jeremy stopped me when we reached the base of the stairs. "What?"

"I was talking to Sawyer," I said. "And—"

"Robison? Are you cheating on me, Jacks?"

Jeremy frowned deeply at me, though there was a twinkle in his eye. However, he seemed genuinely hurt for some reason.

"Hardly," I said. "He was telling me about the homes and businesses that are serviced by well water got hydrogen sulfide—or something—in the water. Sulfur bacteria. Blah blah blah. It's made the water smell like rotten eggs. It's was really noticeable in pipes that aren't used as often. I noticed the smell at your house when I dropped off your cards. I had to make a quick pit stop before I left."

"Ah. Okay," Jeremy said. "So, you were just snooping all over my house? Helping yourself to all of my facilities?"

Jeremy had made the accusation in jest, teasing me about my visit to his house, but something in what he said struck me. Instead of heading up the stairs when he nudged me again, I decided I had one last thing to mention to him.

"I never noticed that painting in your living room before," I said.

Jeremy had been about to nudge me towards the stairs by poking me in the ribs, but he stopped and stared at me. A moment passed before he spoke.

"What painting?" he asked nonchalantly.

Frowning, I gave him a look that let him know I didn't believe he was confused.

"The *only* painting in your living room," I said. "The one behind your comfy chair close to the front door."

"Oh," Jeremy said, waving me off, "that's just a painting. No big deal."

He tried to push me up the stairs.

"Where'd you get it?" I asked, standing my ground.

"Why does it matter, Jacks?" he asked, chuckling. "Less décor talk and more eating of food. Let's go!"

"Because it looks like Prescott Pemberton's work," I said before I could stop myself.

I stopped talking immediately, realizing how what I'd said sounded. Instead of making casual conversation about a piece of art in my best friend's house, it would appear to anyone that I was accusing him of something. I cleared my throat and tried again.

"It matches the style of his artwork I found online," I said. "It also looks like Toulouse-Lautrec's work—or style—but as far as I know, *he* never lived in Head Rock Harbor."

I chuckled, hoping it softened what I was saying.

Jeremy frowned deeply and wouldn't meet my eyes.

"Is…is it one of Prescott's paintings?" I asked.

"Yes," he said, stepping back.

"Why do you—"

"I know, I know," Jeremy said. "I should have mentioned it to Marv. Having a connection to someone whose death I investigated is a moral gray area. But…Jacks…I'd have a connection to anyone in this town, right? It's no big deal."

"A…*connection?*" I asked. "What are you…what kind of connection?"

Jeremy cringed, avoiding my eyes for a moment. When he finally looked at me, I caught on to what he was implying.

"Seriously?" I grumbled. "Really, Germ? Is there not a single guy in this town you haven't put the moves on? Prescott could have been your father. Or mine!"

Jeremy blushed and looked down, though I wasn't sure if he was embarrassed or upset.

"So," I asked, "was the painting payment for services? A lover's gift? Or did you...help yourself to it one night while you were at his house?"

"Wow," Jeremy finally looked up at me, heat in his eyes. "Wow, Jacks."

"I'm sorry," I said. "But you have to realize how this looks. You have a Prescott Pemberton painting in your living room, he's dead, you investigated his death, and you didn't bother to tell anyone, including your chief, that you had an...*intimate* relationship with the deceased. Not to mention one of his paintings that is worth a lot of money. Even more money *now*."

"It was no one's business!" Jeremy grumbled and turned away, stalking towards the front door.

"It's your chief's business," I said, following him. "You don't want to tell me about your personal life, that's fine. You don't have to. We've only been best friends since kindergarten. But Marv should have been told."

"Give it a rest, Jacks," Jeremy shrugged me off as he flipped the lock on the front door.

I put my hand on the door, keeping him from opening it.

"We can't find any paintings of Prescott's," I said. "His sister seemed to think he was painting up a storm, but there're no paintings to be found. But you have one casually hanging on your wall. That's definitely something Marv would be interested in, Jeremy."

"What are you accusing me of?" he asked, turning to me with red cheeks.

"Nothing," I said. "Except withholding important information about your professional integrity and a conflict of interest."

"Get lost, Jacks," Jeremy pulled the door open.

I grabbed his shoulder.

"When did you get the painting?" I asked quickly before he could leave.

"Not that it matters—or is any of your business—but, like, nine months ago," Jeremy shrugged my hand off. "He *gave* it to me. I'm gonna go eat at Munchies. *Friend*."

Then he was gone, and I was left holding the door as the early Spring air slapped against my cheeks. Finally, I shook my head clear of thoughts and closed and locked the door. After taking a few deep breaths to clear my head further, I headed back to the stairs and made my way up to my apartment.

I went to my fridge and scooped up some leftovers onto a plate and popped it into the microwave. My stomach was rumbling from hunger, but I wasn't sure if I was all that hungry anymore.

"*Meow*." Rattlesnatches was on my bed, staring at me with reproach.

"Yeah," I said with a sigh. "I know. I've got a big mouth."

CHAPTER SIXTEEN

In the end, the bookstore got closed an hour earlier than it typically did on a Thursday night. The reasons were many and varied. One, the roaring river of customers had slowed to a mere trickle by six o'clock. Two, I wanted to get back up to the Pemberton place to spray some room deodorizer in his studio and make sure the smell in the pipes was flushed away. Third, and finally, I had merely picked at my lunch, so my stomach was grumbly angrily at me.

By the time I'd run upstairs to make sure Rattlesnatches had food in his bowl, grabbed the room deodorizer from under the kitchen sink, and made my way back downstairs, my stomach was waging a war. I flipped the lights off at the front door and exited the shop hastily, locking up tightly behind me. Out on the street, I held a hand to my stomach, trying to calm it down. I wanted to make it up to the Pemberton place before dinner, otherwise I'd be driving up and down the hillside in pitch darkness.

As I turned to walk around the side of the shop, I caught movement further down the street out of the corner of my eye. I turned in time to see Jeremy walking out of Munchies towards the chief's cruiser. Marv was right behind him, coming out of the door of the café. They walked across the street to police cruiser, and Jeremy headed to the driver's door, intent on taking the wheel.

Marv seemed to be fine with Jeremy driving the cruiser, and walked around to the passenger side. Jeremy stood at the driver's side, lifting and lowering the handle on the door sheepishly. Marv shook his head, reached into his pocket and tossed his keys over the roof of the car to Jeremy. After the car was unlocked, the two of them climbed in and took off down Harbor Street.

He's always forgetting his keys, I thought.

I'd nearly hollered out to Jeremy when I'd first seen him exit Munchies, but I was glad I hadn't done it. Having to apologize to him in front of Marv—especially given the thing I'd be apologizing for—was not something I would have relished. However, I didn't want to apologize simply for essentially accusing him of impropriety—or worse—earlier in the day. I also wanted to apologize for basically making him get two meals in one day from Munchies.

Not that Munchies didn't have delicious food, but having to eat at a restaurant for the two major meals of the day was depressing. Not to mention expensive. However, not enough time had passed, and the opportunity hadn't been good to apologize. Eventually, I'd corner Jeremy when he was alone and atone for what I'd done to upset him. With my stomach grumbling and needing to get to the Pemberton place, it was easy to push it to the back of my mind.

I hopped in my car, a 1992 fire engine red Volkswagen Beetle, which, like the bookstore, also belonged to my aunt while she was alive. However, the thing still ran like a dream thirty years after it was produced, so I saw no sense in swapping it out for something newer. Until the tires fell off, I was going to drive the hand-me-down car for as long as I could.

Puttering up the bluff, I rolled the windows down to enjoy the cool early evening air. Though it was still a bit chilly, I could tell that warmer days were around the corner. It can get bitterly cold in Head Rock Harbor during our winters, but summer is rarely scorching. Mid-80s are usually the worst we have to deal with, even at the peak of our hottest season. So, looking forward to warm weather in Head Rock Harbor isn't crazy.

Thinking about the weather made me wonder why anyone would want to live up on the bluff. During summer, you could probably survive without air conditioning if you left all your windows open. The breeze coming off the river would likely keep your house nice and cool. However, in winter, you'd be exposed to the icy air from the river as well. You'd also have to risk driving the treacherous road up and down the bluff anytime you left or came home.

Snow is common in Head Rock Harbor during winter, especially right before Christmas through the end of January. Ice was rare. However, compacted snow that didn't get plowed and the rare ice storm would make Bluff Road a harrowing drive. If I lived on the bluff, I'd probably stock up my house with food at the end of November and wait the season out. Of course, no one that I knew of had ever encountered problems with living on the bluff, so Bluff Road obviously wasn't all that dangerous in winter, no matter how it looked.

At the Pemberton place, I parked the Beetle parallel to the front door, grabbed my keys and the deodorizer and hopped out of the car. Seconds later, I was entering the house, using the key that Charlene had given me and I hadn't returned. Unfortunately, in my haste, I didn't get the lock on the first try and nearly plowed into the door trying to open it. Another try and I got the door unlocked and open. It struck me immediately that the front entryway and hallway lights were on. I began to wonder if I had left the lights on from two days prior when Sawyer and I had come to investigate the smell in the studio.

I had been certain that I'd turned off all the lights and locked up when I left, but it dawned on me that I could have been in a rush to leave and forgotten to turn off the entry lights. I made a mental note to double check everything when I left again. Certainly, Prescott's sister and mother would be responsible for any utility bills, now that Prescott was gone, and I didn't want to make their situation worse by running up the electricity usage.

Taking the stairs two at a time, I made my way upstairs, then down the hall to the studio. As soon as I entered the room, I found that I'd left the light on in there as well. Slapping myself in the forehead as punishment, I then gave the room a healthy sniff. Fortunately, the rotten egg smell was mostly gone, though a residual fishy smell remained. However, it was slight, and had gotten much better since the day we'd run the water and flushed the toilet.

I didn't have time to open the windows and let the room air out, so I began spraying the deodorizer all over the studio, making sure to avoid the canvas on the easel. I couldn't imagine that the barely started painting would be of use to anyone, but I didn't want to ruin it either way. Moving into the bathroom, I created a cloud of deodorizer in the closet-sized room, nearly choking myself on the mist that emanated from the bottle.

Choking and laughing at myself, I started to duck out of the bathroom. However, as I began to step back into the studio, I noticed that the pile of clothes that had been in the corner of the bathroom during my prior visit was gone. I spun around, looking all over, as though the miniscule bathroom had any hiding places, but could not find the clothes.

With a frown, I exited the bathroom, making certain I turned off the light. I let my eyes linger over every inch of the studio as I stood there, but the clothes hadn't moved themselves to some other corner. Not that clothes were capable of such things. Shrugging, I went over to the pile of art supplies and towels in the corner under the windows.

I pushed things around and lifted canvases and other items enough to make sure the clothes hadn't somehow found their way into the pile. All I found was blank canvases, a spare easel, tubes of oil paints, a box of brushes, a jug of paint thinner, a glass amber bottle crudely labeled as aniline, and some white towels that had absorbed the former unpleasant stench of the room. I quickly gave them a blast from the deodorizer, hoping it would help exorcise the smell from the room.

My stomach was grumbling angrily at me, so I gave the room one last crop dusting from the bottle of deodorizer and exited. I double checked that all the lights were off in the studio. Next, I checked all the upstairs rooms to make sure the lights were off, then made my way downstairs. To be certain, I checked the kitchen, den, downstairs bathroom, dining room, and parlor to make sure the lights were off.

Then I made my way to the front hall, turned off the light, and exited the house. I double checked the door after I locked it, making sure the knob didn't turn once the door was shut.

Satisfied that I had done a thorough job of deodorizing the room and that I'd turned off all the lights and locked up the house, I hopped back in the Beetle. The trip down Bluff Road with the wind blowing my hair was delightful, but my stomach didn't care. It wanted food above all things. Crispy spring air scented by freshly budding trees didn't interest my stomach any.

A quick two-minute car ride down Bluff Road and across town and I was parking outside of Harper's. I had intended to drop my car off at the bookstore and walk to Harper's, then walk home after dinner, but my stomach would hear none of it. I wouldn't be getting my evening exercise in, but instead giving into my stomach's wishes. Being on the tail end of dinner and the cusp of the drinking hour, I made sure to lock the Beetle. I didn't want any drunks doing weird things with my car if they stumbled out of Harper's while I was eating.

Inside, I was surprised to see the dining room completely full. Apparently, people were dragging out dinner before moving into the bar area. Heidi gave me an apologetic grin and a shrug as I stood there, staring at the lack of seating desperately.

"I'll be in the bar," I said. "I'll eat there."

"Okay, hun," she said.

I sauntered over the bar, primed to give Cleo my order immediately, only to find Deb sitting on one of the stools, smoking a cigarette, one leg on the floor, one on the rung of the stool. From the looks of things—especially the cigarette during the dinner rush—told me she had been drinking. Heavily. The way her flannel was hanging off one shoulder, exposing her bra strap further proved my theory. That was Deb in a nutshell. Sometimes she did good. Sometimes she did bad. Thursday night was going to be a bad night.

I sidled up to the bar, exchanging a concerned look with Cleo, before hopping up onto the stool next to Deb.

"Could I get a cheesesteak and rings?" I asked loudly to be heard over the noise. "To go?"

Cleo gave me a nod, then her eyes flicked to Deb and back to me. I shrugged. Cleo went over to tap my order into the machine.

"Well," Deb slurred, finally noticing me, "if it isn't the fruit of my loins. How are you this evening, loin fruit?"

I turned my head to stare at my mother for a moment. Her lipstick was slightly smudged. One of her eyelashes was coming off at the corner, and her eyes looked glazed over—even though she was smiling.

"Have you had a few tonight, Deb?" I asked.

Deb glared at me for a moment, then turned to Cleo.

"Did you know this one," she said, jabbing her thumb at me, "didn't speak for the first three years of his life?"

Cleo shook her head politely and went about pouring a draft beer. I stared at Deb.

"S'true," Deb slurred. "Didn't say a single word for three years. Then, one night, his daddy and I got into a fight. Big one. Huge. We was fussin' and fightin' and hollerin' and he hit me, so I hit him, and it spilled out of the trailer and into the yard. It was raining somethin' fierce. Cold."

Cleo was listening politely, but I could tell she was uncomfortable. I knew the story, so I was unbothered.

However, I was concerned about my mother slipping up on her drinking again. I could no longer be embarrassed, but she was embarrassing herself.

"Well," Deb continued, taking a drag off of her smoke, "the cops show up. Probably that damn Mavis who called 'em. She doesn't want anyone to steal her thunder. Anyway, just as they pull up and get out of their cars, I pushed this one's daddy into a huge mud puddle. He gets stuck, starts flailing around—"

Deb took the final drag off her smoke, then used it to light another Newport, took a deep drag, then launched back into her story.

"—actin' a dang fool, makin' all kinds of noise. Threatening to kill everyone. Even the cops. This one here, standing on the porch in just his feetie jammies looks at the cops and says '*Do y'all not see this?*'" Deb finished her story with a cackle. "First time he said anything was a full sentence. Probably was able to talk since he was six months old but didn't bother. Even then he knew he was better than us."

Cleo gave her a polite chuckle as she shot me a sympathetic look, then went back to pouring beers.

"Been better than us ever since," Deb stated bitterly, though the smile didn't leave her face. "Isn't that right, loin fruit?"

"You got someone to get you home later?" I asked, ignoring the question.

"I can take care m'self."

"Can you?" I asked. "When did that start?"

Deb slapped her hand on the bar so hard Cleo jumped and the two men playing pool looked over in shock. I was unstartled.

"I been takin' care m'self since you was fourteen years old," she said.

"You had to," I said. "I gave up the gig to live with Aunt Belinda. Anyway—"

Deb was glaring at me.

"—you gonna get home okay later?"

"I'll make sure of it," Cleo answered to keep Deb from tearing into me.

"Thanks," I said, giving her a smile before turning my attention back to my mother.

"Don't give me that look," Deb growled.

"What look?"

"That judgmental look you always give me when I decide to have a good time."

"I wouldn't judge you if your good time didn't come at the expense of others."

"You look here you—"

"No, Deb," I said. "I'm not going to fight with you. I'm sorry I said anything. Just drop it. I'm not doing this. I've done this enough. You have your drinks and Cleo can get you home and I'll mind my business. Okay?"

"Fine," Deb bit the word off.

"Good," I said.

We sat in silence for several minutes as Cleo made conversation with people who came up to the bar for drinks, served them, and ignored us. I couldn't blame her. Deb smoked her Newports and I waited patiently on my food. I desperately wanted to say something to Deb about her drinking and her behavior, but I'd been doing it my entire life. Sometimes you have to let people be who they are, no matter how it makes you feel.

Right when I thought I might start to scream about why my food was taking so long—my stomach was grumbling again—Deb nudged me. I looked over at her and at my arm, making sure she hadn't gotten any cigarette ash on me. Fortunately, her cigarette was in her other hand. Deb was looking at the other end of the bar area by the pool tables.

"Germ deserves better," she said, slurring.

"What?" I asked.

"That's that *Billy* over there." She jabbed her cigarette towards the other end of the bar. "He just slithered in."

"Who?" I asked, turning to look.

"That boy he's been seeing from out of town," Deb mumbled. "Germ must be workin' the night shift."

"Why do you say that?" I asked, my eyes landing on a youngish guy with dark hair, standing at the end of the bar, talking to another guy about my age.

"Every time he's worked at night for the last few weeks, that boy comes in here flirtin' with all the men who will tolerate it," Deb spat. "Pitiful."

I said nothing about things that I found pitiful, but instead watched the guy for a few moments. He was an attractive young guy, like Jeremy, but he was definitely flirting. I had no idea if Jeremy would be bothered by that, so I didn't know if it was worth getting upset over.

"Well," I said, "it's none of my business."

Deb snorted. "Yeah. You're known for mindin' your business."

"Cleo?" I asked more loudly than needed. "Is my food almost up?"

Cleo, startled, jerked and looked towards the passthrough to the kitchen.

"I think Beau is putting it in the window now, Jackson," she said. "I'll go grab it."

"Thanks," I said.

Deb was smoking and glaring at the side of my face, but I stared straight ahead, not giving her the satisfaction of looking back at her. Finally, when Cleo arrived, she passed the brown paper bag across the bar to me. I slapped down a twenty-dollar bill—for the food and a tip—and slid from the stool.

"Your money's no good here," Cleo chuckled.

Deb snatched it off the bar and slid it into her bra. "It is tonight."

Cleo said nothing, but hurriedly went back to serving drinks.

"Have one on me, Deb," I said. "Or several."

Then I exited Harper's as quickly as I could. Driving home and eating my dinner was all I had left that I wanted to do. I wasn't going to think about my mother's issues. Or the problems those issues created for me growing up. I wasn't.

My sleep was fitful that night. And it wasn't because of the cheesesteak and rings.

CHAPTER SEVENTEEN

"You sure you don't want to hold onto it?" Charlene asked as she slipped the key to the Pemberton place back into her purse.

"I'm done," I said. "After looking around and checking things out, I can definitively say that what you should do is an as-is sale of the house and its contents."

Charlene looked disappointed as she closed her purse and stowed it beneath the counter in her shop, and I couldn't blame her. One would expect more exciting news about a famous painter's house up on the bluff in Head Rock Harbor. Unfortunately, though interesting in life, Prescott—and his family—weren't much for ostentations. They're house was gorgeous, but it wasn't filled with pricey baubles or furniture waiting to be sold out for a profit.

I'd stepped next door to Charlene's Chocolates on my lunch break the next day. I wanted to break the official news about the house and contents to her, give her the key and relinquish my responsibility for it, and to warn her about the studio smell. Texting Marv to let him know that I no longer had a key was going to be my next order of business.

Anything to do with Prescott, the Pemberton house, or Marshelle needed to be pushed from my mind.

"That's unfortunate," Charlene said. "I'd hoped…well, we looked everywhere for paintings, didn't we?"

I nodded. "Yeah. Speaking of which, I sprayed some deodorizer around Prescott's studio at the house last night."

Explaining what Sawyer had told me about the pipes, Charlene nodded along, realizing it was a good idea to spray the deodorizer.

"You'll want to go up and open the windows this weekend for a few hours, though," I said. "Really air out the last bit of the smell. I didn't have time for that. I think the smell is mostly gone now, though."

"Well, at least there's some good news," Charlene said. "Even if we couldn't find any paintings, at least the house is sellable. That makes things a bit better, right?"

I stared at her for a moment.

"I'm not certain Prescott would agree," I said, then remembered my new motto, "but what's done is done. I'm sure it'll all work out for you at the auction."

Fortunately for me, Charlene was so consumed with thoughts of not having any dead artist's paintings to auction off that she hadn't heard my snide comment.

"Well," Charlene said, "I appreciate all you've done, Jackson. And for making sure to verify everything in the house is as I said it is."

I felt that was an odd comment for Charlene, but I chose to ignore it. Minding my business was supposed to be my new motto. Not simply because it was the right thing to do— keeping my nose out of places it didn't belong—but it also helped me avoid headaches and stress.

"You're welcome," I said, heading for the door. "I've got one more stop to make during my lunch break, so I've got to scoot. Thanks for loaning me the key."

"Sure thing, Jackson."

Leaving Charlene's shop, I quickly made my way down Harbor Street and cut a left towards Jeremy's house. I'd really wanted to spend my Friday lunch break having an actual lunch, but a snack between customers later would have to do. Returning the key to the Pemberton place to wash my hands of the ordeal was paramount. Apologizing the Jeremy was nearly as important.

By the time I found myself in front of Jeremy's house, clouds had rolled into town, darkening the sky and casting everything in a bluish-gray. The wind off the river had picked up a bit and was tussling my hair as I dashed up the sidewalk to Jeremy's front door. I pulled my jacket tightly around me as I knocked on the front door, hoping my best friend wasn't sleeping. Fortunately, after a few knocks, I heard movement in the house and the lock disengage.

"What are you doing here?" Jeremy asked blandly as he opened the door.

He opened it just far enough for me to tell that he was still in his robe and was unprepared to receive guests. His tone let me know that prepared or not, I was a guest he'd rather not host.

"To beg your pardon," I said, grinning awkwardly as I held my hands up defensively.

Jeremy eyed me warily, but he let the door creak open a bit wider.

"I'm sorry for yesterday," I said, not waiting for him to respond. "I basically implied you had something to do with

Prescott's death. Or that you weren't ethical. Or, at the very least, you were performing your job poorly. I'm sorry."

"You definitely had a lot to say," Jeremy said, the door opening a little more.

"Again, I'm sorry," I said. "I know you well enough to know that you might not be perfect, but you wouldn't intentionally harm anyone."

A ghost of a smile started to form on Jeremy's lips, and he looked ready to say something, but a noise behind him, deep in the house made him glance over his shoulder. I tilted my head to look past him, but Jeremy, turning to see my curiosity, pushed the door back into place and blocked my view.

"Okay," he said quickly. "Apology accepted."

"Got company?" I asked. "Is it Billy? Deb pointed him out last night."

"*Bobby*," Jeremy said, rolling his eyes. "Yeah. I gotta go, Jacks. We'll talk soon. Okay?"

He started to close the door.

"Hey." I placed my hand on the door to stop him. "Did you take anything from the Pemberton place? Or move anything?"

"What?" Jeremy frowned at me.

"I was there last night," I said, keeping my hand on the door. "You, Charlene, and I had keys. And some things were missing from his studio when I was deodorizing it last night. Did you take anything or move anything?"

Jeremy's eyes turned to slits and he glared at me.

"That apology lasted two seconds. Good job, Jacks."

"What?" I asked. "I just meant—"

"Look," he said, pushing my hand off the door, "we can fight later. I don't have time for your accusations right now. Great apology. *Friend.*"

Then he shut the door in my face. Immediately, I heard Jeremy talking with his *company* on the other side of the door, as though Jeremy was explaining his crazy best friend's appearance to his him. With a sigh, I stepped away from the door and made my way back down the sidewalk to the road. Once again, I'd managed to mess up my friendship with Jeremy.

Rattlesnatches would have plenty to say when I got back to the bookstore, I was sure.

CHAPTER EIGHTEEN

Rattlesnatches gave me the cold shoulder the rest of the day. It was if he knew I had run my mouth off once again. I spent the rest of the work day helping customers and mentally chastising myself for my recent behavior. Having a fight with Deb, putting my nose in a million places it didn't belong, practically accusing my best friend of murder and theft; I was batting zero.

Fortunately, business was booming since it was a Friday afternoon, so while I could think about how awful I felt, I was mostly distracted. When my shipment of Harrison Garner books I'd order was delivered right before closing time, that pushed everything else from my mind. They were some of my biggest selling—if not best-selling—books in the store. With the next day being Saturday—a day when tons of customers topped by—I really needed to get the books out on display before the night was over.

Since I knew that my evening was dedicated to the Harrison Garner books, and Rattlesnatches had no use for me, I decided to treat myself for dinner. Not cooking wasn't that uncommon for me. However, skipping Munchies and Harper's in favor of something else was. I decided to join all of Head Rock Harbor's most influential citizens and all of the wide-eyed tourists at The Dock.

As luck would have it, the clouds that had rolled into town during lunch lingered for the rest of the day. When I was driving up The Dock in the Beetle, the misty rain was beginning. Due to the weather, the main draw of The Dock—outdoor seating on the deck—was ruined. Only the hardcore townies who loved the food seemed to be showing up for Friday dinner. The tourists were choosing other places to dine for the first night of the weekend.

So, when I found myself at a two-top near the window and enjoying a glass of Chardonnay and my appetizer of mini crab cakes twenty minutes after arriving, I was pleased. The window seat didn't have the best view, considering the weather, but having no one to talk to over dinner made watching the rain a fascinating activity.

With the rain producing a smaller than usual crowd on what should have been a busy Friday night, the waitstaff were allowing diners more time to enjoy themselves. I wasn't rushed through my appetizer and drink, forced to decide on a main within minutes of eating my first crab cake. Having a relaxing dinner at a leisurely pace, watching the rain, and enjoying my wine, I found that most of my worries were slowly sloughing away.

After I finished my appetizer, and nearly the entire first glass of wine, I decided to switch things up. I ordered a medium rare porterhouse for my main with asparagus and Dauphinoise potatoes as my sides. To go along with dinner, I asked to be switched to a peppery Merlot. Even though I knew the bill for dinner was going to be much more than I had intended to spend when I first came up with the idea of eating at The Dock, I didn't care. I was chasing away worries.

I was nearly done with my chardonnay, waiting on my steak, when someone clearing their throat at my tableside drew my attention from watching the rain through the window. When I turned, expecting to see my waiter with my food, I instead found Linda Wagner looking down at me. Nearly choking on the sip of my wine I was taking, I set my glass down and wiped my mouth with my napkin.

"Linda," I said.

"I was just on my way to the powder room," she said, glancing off towards the restrooms, "and saw you sitting here. It's not often I see you here."

"Even those of us on the lower rungs of society like a steak once in a while."

Linda ignored my snide comment.

"Everything is just wonderful here," she said, as though it was my first time experiencing The Dock's food. "Mark and I are here every Friday."

Linda spoke to me as though I hadn't lived in Head Rock Harbor my entire life and didn't know the mayor and her husband were regulars at the nicest restaurant in town. Fortunately, the chardonnay had softened my disposition, so I didn't say something snide a second time.

"I'm enjoying it," I said.

"Mm," Linda said. "Have you given any more thought to what we discussed?"

Linda crossed her arms over her chest and stared down at me. As I stared up at her, I realized there wasn't enough chardonnay in the world to ever agree to our mayor's demand that I organize a Pride parade. However, I didn't want to ruin my meal—or the rest of my evening.

"I'm always thinking about something," I said.

And it was the truth. Linda seemed to be satisfied with that answer for the time being.

"Well," she said, moving on, "have you and Charlene decided what to do about the Pemberton place? It's been a while, hasn't it?"

Frowning, I wasn't quite sure what to say to Linda. She really had no stake in what happened to the Pemberton house. Telling her anything about what Charlene and I had talked about or done to the place didn't seem quite right. Not giving Linda some kind of answer to any question she asked was never a viable course of action, though. Unless you wanted to find yourself dealing with even more questions.

"I'm not really involved anymore," I said. "But I think it has been decided—between Charlene and the family—that the house will be sold at auction as-is. There's not really much in the house to auction off, so that seems best."

"That seems fair," Linda said. "And what of the paintings?"

I cocked my head to the side, confused.

"*Prescott Pemberton's paintings*," Linda groaned as if I was the densest person she ever met. "Charlene had said that the family might donate one to the town for all of her help. We could auction it off and put the money towards something important. Like fixing up the library, or—"

"What paintings?" I interjected.

Linda just stared down at me. Her mouth was still half-open from when I interrupted her.

"Prescott didn't have any paintings in the house," I said. "I don't know what Charlene promised you, but—"

"She said at the beginning that there would be tons of paintings!" Linda snapped. "You're telling me there aren't *any* paintings?"

I slowly shook my head. "We haven't found a single one. Not even a finished one that's been hanging on a wall in the house. All we found was one that had barely been started. And that's being generous."

Linda rolled her eyes dramatically.

"I'll just have a talk with little miss Charlene, won't I?"

Then she stomped away towards the bathrooms. As she disappeared, my waiter appeared with my food and my glass of Merlot. He set my plates in front of me, along with the glass, checked to make sure I was good, then disappeared once more. As I cut off the first bite of my steak, I was left wondering why Charlene was so certain we'd find 'a ton' of paintings.

And why hadn't she told Linda that she was wrong? We'd known that for quite some time.

CHAPTER NINETEEN

For all the judgement I'd cast on my mother the previous night, I was embarrassed to admit that I arrived back to the bookstore a little more inebriated than I had intended to be. The fact that I drove the Beetle home was not something of which I was proud. Fortunately, Marv, Jeremy, and Officer Riley didn't run across the path I cut back to the bookstore, so further embarrassment was avoided. Aside from the look Rattlesnatches gave me when I stumbled into the bookstore, soaked from the rain, I'd avoided most of the pratfalls of having too much to drink when out for dinner.

Of course, in my slightly buzzed stupor, I realized I still had to work on a Harrison Garner display before the shop could open the next day. Unable to find my boxcutter, I'd gone up to my apartment and retrieved a butcher knife from the kitchen. Using it to open the boxes of books at the check-out counter, I knew I'd probably ruined the knife. Setting up the book display was more important than the tool I used to chop onions, though.

Minutes after setting the knife on the check-out counter and hauling the handful of boxes over to the other side of the bookstore, I found myself sitting cross-legged on the floor,

Surrounded by the five open boxes, the books inside peeking out at me, I really wanted to lie down and go to sleep. Between the wine, the food, and the stress of the last few days, I didn't know if I had the energy to make a display of books—even for best-selling ones.

"Meow." Rattlesnatches sauntered by, bumping me with his noggin and rubbing the length of his body across my side.

"Yeah," I said. "I know. I'm going to do it."

I could always depend on my Rattlesnatches to crack the whip when I was slacking off. He sat back on his haunches, looked up and me, and blinked. Obviously, he was trying to convey that the quicker I put the display together, the sooner we'd be snuggled up in bed. Sighing, I realized that he was right. The longer I sat there, feeling sorry for myself, the later it would be before we were in bed. And the more tired I'd be opening the shop the next day.

Pulling the first few books out of the box closest to me, I got to work. My buzz was starting to dissipate, and it reminded me that I'd be lucky if I didn't have a wine headache the next day. Hangovers and headaches were the two big reasons I rarely drank. Familial alcoholism was the most important reason I rarely drank. Of course, with how easily I got a hangover from just a few drinks, it would have probably been impossible for me to entertain becoming an alcoholic.

I'd be a poor one if I tried.

Thunder rumbled outside as the rain picked up, making its "tickety-tackety" sound on the front windows and the front door of the shop. The overhead lights flickered briefly when a rather powerful roll of thunder shot through the sky, but didn't go out. I couldn't help but wonder if someone wasn't telling me to go to bed and get up early to complete the display. However, Rattlesnatches was unbothered by the weather and continued to sit there, staring at me, urging me to work on the display.

"*Meow.*"

Rattlesnatches jerked as another violent roll of thunder shook the store. I chuckled and reached over to scratch the top of his head as another flash of lightning shot through the sky.

"Looks like we're in for an all-nighter," I said to him, still scratching. "The rain will make for good sleeping."

Rattlesnatches, though enamored with the way I was scratching behind his ears, gave me a disbelieving look. I couldn't blame him. The thunder was violent enough that I wasn't certain it wouldn't keep us awake if it continued on all night. I love thunder, but it's not conducive to restfulness when it sounds like whip cracks overhead.

I pulled the rest of the books out of the box and moved onto the next with my free hand as I continued to scratch Rattlesnatches' noggin. As I pulled books, he enjoyed the attention. After a few moments however, though he didn't move his head from under my fingers, Rattlesnatches alerted, his head twisting around to look towards the front of the shop.

My hand that was digging through boxes froze on the spine of the next book I was going to remove from the box, but my fingers kept scratching Rattlesnatches' head. Both of us stared towards the front of the shop, our view blocked by the rows of bookcases. As another crack of thunder whipped through the sky overhead, I could have sworn I heard the bell over the door chime.

Rattlesnatches pulled away immediately and leapt, climbing the True Crime bookshelf, obviously having heard the bell, too. He wanted to scope out if what we heard was an auditory illusion or someone actually entering the shop.

I'd locked the door. Hadn't I? Had I come back to the shop so drunk that I made such a careless mistake, such as leave the front door to the shop unlocked?

It was possible that someone saw the lights on and was coming in to shop for a book. However, remembering the storm outside, and hearing the rain pound on the windows, made a tingle run up my spine. I nearly called out, questioning who had entered the shop, asking them to identify themselves. However, I suddenly remembered that no one reasonable would be out shopping on a night like tonight.

I started to rise from my spot on the floor when Rattlesnatches meowed down at me from the top of the bookcase. Then the lights flicked off. Startled, I jerked, nearly coming out of my skin, almost climbing the bookcase to join Rattlesnatches on top of it. Even though the storm was still raging, I could hear the distinct sound of footsteps walking through the shop by the check-out counter.

Rattlesnatches leapt away from the top of the True Crime bookshelf and out of sight. Not that he had been more than an inky shadow with the lights off. The shop became shades of deep navy blue and inky blackness, illuminated periodically by the flashes of lightning outside. I ducked behind the corner of True Crime bookshelf and inched my way forward, keeping my back to the books.

Someone was in the shop near the check-out counter— and I needed to find out who it was. As I inched my way along the length of the bookshelf, eyes opened wide for any sign of a human-sized shadow coming around the corner, I listened for footsteps. They stopped somewhere around the front of the check-out counter, though I wasn't certain I could trust my ears. My head was still a little fuzzy from dinner, and hearing is not the best judge of distance.

When I heard the sound of metal sliding along the check-out counter, I froze. I'd chopped enough vegetables and prepared enough dinners to know the sound of a knife dragging along wood. Whoever had entered the shop had found my butcher knife on the counter. I was no expert, but I knew two things in that moment.

A customer entering a bookstore to shop wouldn't turn off the lights.

That same person would not feel the need to pick up the nearest deadly weapon.

Whoever was inside Head Rock Harbor Books had come with an agenda.

My chest was threatening to heave, sending great puffs of air out of my lungs as anxiety began to overtake me. Thinking about what it would mean if I made that much noise, I somehow calmed myself down enough that I could breathe normally as I listened for more movement from the intruder. I kept my back against the bookshelf as I listened carefully to the sounds of the shop. Thunder cracked. Lightning flashed. And the store was silent otherwise.

Right when I thought I'd go crazy from standing so rigidly in such a position for so long, the footsteps started up again. They were moving from the check-out counter towards the stairs up to my apartment. My eyes darted to the balcony above that overlooked the shop. I'd left the apartment door open when I'd gone up to retrieve the butcher knife. Obviously, the intruder assumed I was upstairs, and they were headed up to find me. With a knife. If that didn't spell out their intentions, I didn't know what would.

I began to inch backwards, keeping my back against the shelf as I made my way farther away from the stairs. It dawned on me that if I could back up all the way down the bookshelf, round the corner, then cut across the store, I could creep along the Classics section as the intruder made their way up the stairs, and I could duck out the front door. Even if they heard me exit, I could take off running down the street. There's no way someone with discretion on their mind would chase me down a public street in the middle of the night.

Was there?

I also had to think about Rattlesnatches. Would he follow me? Or would he at least keep out of harm's way atop the shelves until I could get help? Thinking about the possibility that he might do something stupid in an attempt to help me made me pause. Could I leave him alone in the bookstore while I ran for help? Would the intruder even care about harming my cat?

Knowing I didn't have time to think every single scenario through, I started backing up again, right as the first step sounded on the stairs. Inching further away, I made my way towards the other end of the True Crime bookshelf. If I timed things just right, I could be rounding the bookshelf and slinking towards the front of the store, passing by the open aisles created by the bookshelves as the intruder made their way upstairs.

My plan was perfect. As the intruder made their way towards the apartment, I'd make my way out of the store. If I was really quiet, I might even be able to get out of the bookstore without them knowing it. The thunder and rain might cover the sounds of my exit, especially if I didn't open the door widely enough to hit the bell and squeezed out.

Unfortunately, with all the thoughts and planning going through my head, I made a mistake. Right as the footsteps reached the middle of the staircase, I hit a snag. Having forgotten the pile of books I'd made from unpacking the boxes, my right heel caught the corner of a pile. Backwards I fell, appendages flailing, a sharp gasp escaping my mouth, as I tumbled to the floor loudly.

Footsteps raced down the stairs and towards me. I looked up in time to see the inky shadow of a human race down the True Crime aisle and lunge at me. Quickly, I pushed from the floor and raced around the bookshelf and into the next aisle. The sound of metal scraping on the wood floor told me that I had barely missed becoming a kebab.

I'd barely made it down the aisle, racing towards the front of the store when the footsteps started up behind me again. The intruder was chasing after me, and I had to assume still had possession of the butcher knife, prepared to stab me. When I reached the end of the aisle, instead of turning towards the front door and trying to beat the intruder in a foot race, I ducked to the right. I pushed my back against the bookcase endcap and waited.

When the racing footsteps grew closer, I waited, my breath coming in heaving gusts. As the inky shadow raced out of the aisle, I lunged forward and plowed into the intruder, shoving them roughly. The intruder tumbled head over heels towards the front door. The lightning flashed again, briefly illuminating the human laying by the front door.

Out of the corner of my eye, I saw Rattlesnatches leap down from the Classics section to the base of the door. As the intruder was prying themselves off the floor, Rattlesnatches leapt and swiped at the light switch. He missed on the first try, but as the intruder rose to their feet, Rattlesnatches leapt once more. I had just enough time to face off against the intruder in the dark as they stood before me in shadows.

Right as the lights flickered on with Rattlesnatches' assistance, the intruder spun and dashed out the door, the bell overhead clanging loudly. I barely had time to see the yellow raincoat disappear into the darkness outside.

Without taking time to think, I raced over and locked the front door. I grabbed the stool from behind the check-out counter and wedged it under the doorknob, my chest heaving as I tried to catch my breath. Rattlesnatches was sitting at the base of the door, staring up at me. Quickly, I slapped the lights off and closed the plastic light switch cover.

"*Good job, bud,*" I whispered.

Rattlesnatches leapt up onto the window ledge by the front door, and together, we stared out into the pouring rain as we stood in the darkness of the shop. Even with the lightning flashes periodically, it was impossible to see where the intruder might have gone. The rain wasn't letting up and the thunder was as angry as it had been all night.

I gave up on the Harrison Garner display. Rattlesnatches and I went up to the apartment, locking the door behind us. I rolled the fridge over in front of the door as extra precaution. I have no idea when the storm let up, but it was still going strong when we reluctantly fell asleep an hour later, huddled in bed together.

CHAPTER TWENTY

"So," Marv said, frowning at me as I worked on the display, "let me get this straight."

The locksmith's drill whirred over by the front door, filling the store with a grinding sound. Marv grimaced, but I'd gotten used to it already. After the night I had, it was hard to bother me, anyway.

"Someone broke in here last night—"

"Possibly broke in," I said. "I'm not certain I'd actually locked the door."

"—and tried to attack you with a butcher knife you left on the counter over there," he continued, "but you just went to bed and thought you'd call me this morning?"

"I don't know if 'break in' is the right term," I said. "Nothing was broken. They didn't smash a window or pry the door open with a crowbar, I mean."

"Mmhm," Marv said, his frown deepening. "Jackson, don't take this the wrong way, but are you out of your ever-lovin' mind?"

I couldn't help but grin at that as I continued stacking books on the display. The store was going to open in less than a half hour and I had plenty to do. Get the locksmith to change the lock, finish the display, and give Marv a full report on the intruder situation. My mind was running ninety-to-nothing with theories and unanswered questions, so focusing on any one task was impossible.

"Sorry, Marv," I said. "I'm just...I guess I'm still in shock. Nearly getting murdered will do that, you know?"

Marv's expression softened, but his frown wasn't chased away entirely.

"I understand that, Jackson," he said. "But you should have called me last night. Immediately."

"It was raining," I said, shrugging.

Marv groaned.

"Well," Marv said, stepping around the display to bring himself closer to me, "if you *did* lock the door, is there someone else with a key? That could narrow down who this was...don't you think?"

Nodding, I had to agree with that logic. Marv was actually doing a good job as a police officer, all on his own. Unfortunately, only two people had a key to the front door of the shop. And I didn't want Marv to know who had the spare key.

"Just me," I said.

I immediately hated myself. I couldn't help but wonder if I hadn't sealed my own fate with one little omission. Everything from the night before was racing through my mind. If I had locked the door, the person with the spare key had easily let themselves into the shop. That person also, somehow, decided the best place to find me in the shop once the lights were off, was upstairs in my apartment. It had to be someone who knew about the shop and my routine.

That meant only one thing. Or...*one person.*

However, *why* would that person do such a thing to me? I needed to answer that question before I said anything to Marv about the key and my suspicions.

"Well, that doesn't help," Marv scratched his chin. "And you can't be sure if you locked the door or not?"

"No," I said, shaking the thoughts from my head. "I'm not certain. See, I had a few drinks with my dinner at The Dock last night. I was a little fuzzy."

Marv nodded slowly. Fortunately, he didn't ask me how I got home from dinner. I didn't want to lie to the chief of police more than was necessary.

"One more question, Jackson," Marv said, leaning in. "Why are you changing the locks if you have the only key?"

I'd thought of that question myself, though I never expected Marv to come up with it on his own. Without missing a beat, I gave him the answer I'd already formulated.

"Can't be too cautious, can I?" I said. "If spending a hundred bucks gives me peace of mind, so be it."

Marv harrumphed, but jotted something down in his notebook. I continued to arrange the Harrison Garner display as he jotted, read, jotted some more, then read his notes some more. Obviously, like me, he had a million and one questions and theories racing through his head. However, Marv couldn't quite seem to figure out what he wanted to say or phrase the questions the way he wanted to phrase them.

"So," he said finally, "why call me at all?"

That was a question I hadn't expected.

"What do you mean?" I asked.

"Well," Marv said, crossing his arms over his chest, "nothing was stolen. No one was actually hurt. You felt safe enough to go to bed right after the incident. No one had a spare key and nothing was broken. Why did you call to report it?"

"In case it happens again," I said. "I want a paper trail. And if more break-ins start happening in shops around here, you'll have a record."

Marv harrumphed again, but his arms stayed laced across his chest.

"There's something you're lying about, Jackson Harper," he said. "Or something you're just not telling me."

"Marv," I said, "I told you play by play what happened here last night. I didn't leave anything out."

Jeremy having the only other key to the bookstore was an omission, not a lie. Okay. It was a lie. But it didn't necessarily have anything to do with the incident. Not that I could prove, anyway.

"We'll see," Marv said. "I'm gonna start poking around and you'll find out I can be just as nosy as you. And I can ask just as good questions as you do."

I chuckled. "Marv. This isn't a contest. Police Chief versus an amateur busybody. Honestly, I just wanted you to know in case anything else happened. I swear."

Shaking his head, he closed his little spiral notebook and returned it to his breast pocket. Marv gave me a good looking over, as though he was somehow going to compel me with the use of some type of telepathy to tell him more. My mind and my mouth—for once—were like a steel trap. Even though I had well-founded suspicions, I wasn't going to say anything more to Marv until I was certain I was right.

I'd done enough damage to my friendship with Jeremy by running my mouth. I wanted to be sure that running my mouth one final time was right.

"Well," Marv said, "if you think of anything else, let me know."

"I will," I said as I laid the last book in place on the display.

"And if you want to tell me what you're keeping to yourself," Marv added, giving me a look, "you know where to find me."

With that, he turned and headed up to the front of the shop. Rattlesnatches was on top of the bookshelf, staring down at him, watching him go. When Marv was at the end of the aisle, a desperate thought entered my head, and I hollered out to him.

"Marv?"

He turned, "Yeah?"

Frowning, I asked, "Marshelle? What was the cause of death?"

He cocked his head to the side, frowning at me.

"Why would you ask that?" he asked. "You saw the accident."

"We both did," I said, nodding.

A small grin played at the corner of Marv's mouth.

"Blunt force trauma to the head," he said. "Which could be from hitting her head on the windshield, of course."

Nodding slowly, I stared at Marv.

"Funny how her head was gashed open but there wasn't any blood on the windshield, huh?" I asked.

He stared at me.

"Not much where we found her, either," I added.

"That is funny, isn't it?" Marv's face was blank, but I could tell he wanted to say something.

"How long had she been dead?" I asked.

Marv grinned again, as though proud of me.

"Twelve hours," he said. "Give or take."

Then he nodded and headed out.

I stood there, wishing I'd told Marv about the owner of the spare key. Because it dawned on me that I was certain I had locked the door when I'd come in from dinner the night before. It occurred to me suddenly that when I couldn't find my boxcutter to open the boxes, I'd checked to make sure I locked the door before I went upstairs to get my butcher knife. I'd laid my set of keys on the kitchen counter after grabbing the knife.

Someone had used a key to get into the shop.

And only one other person had a key.

CHAPTER TWENTY-ONE

"Well, that's hard to say," Rita Johnson's voice sounded tinny in the cordless phone.

With the phone held between my shoulder and ear, I was talking to Prescott Pemberton's sister while ringing up the last customer before lunch.

"I'd have to think on that," she said in my ear. *"Give me a moment, dear."*

"Take your time," I said. "That'll be eighteen seventy-seven."

"What?" Rita asked.

"I was talking to a customer," I said, jovially. "You can ignore that."

I smiled at the customer and they gestured at the credit card machine so I gave them a nod. They ran their card and paid for their books while I balanced the phone and bagged up their purchases. Once I handed their bag and receipt over to them, I followed them to the door and gave them a goodbye wave and smile when I opened the door for them. Then I locked the front door to the shop behind them.

More customers were not going to come in before I could have lunch. Of course, I'd locked the door to the shop the night before and that hadn't stopped someone from entering. Sighing to myself, I wandered back over the check-out counter and cleaned up my messes from the morning as I waited for Rita to hem and haw on the other end of the line.

By the time I'd put away all of my supplies, cleaned up scraps of trash and paper, and straightened up the counter displays, she was still humming to herself. Rattlesnatches was still in his little nest on the check-out counter. He hadn't left my side all day, for which I was grateful. Having him by my side kept my nerves from the night before in check.

"*Well*," Rita spoke up, right as I was about to give up, "*I'd have to say the last few weeks it got worse. At least, that's when Prescott mentioned it most.*"

"So," I said, snapping out of my daydreams, "Prescott was having his headaches, dizzy spells and all that for months before he left New York? And then they cleared up almost immediately after moving here?"

"*Not completely, no,*" Rita said. "*Mostly, though. Maybe once or twice a month he'd complain about a headache or feeling dizzy, but they seemed to be getting better. It seemed a change of scenery alleviated the problems some. It was getting to where he could live with it.*"

"I see," I said. "But the last few weeks before...well, before he passed...he said it had all gotten worse?"

Rita sighed.

"*Yes,*" she said. "*It seemed he couldn't outrun his health problems forever. Then, I guess, he picked up the drinking again to deal with it, and...well...*"

"That's okay," I said, stopping her. "I don't meant to make you talk about more than you're comfortable with, Rita."

"Thank you," she said, sniffling. *"Though I'm still not certain why you are concerned with Prescott's health issues. Seems a little late."*

She gave a small chuckle, so I joined in to be polite. I ignored the question.

"And he said he was working hard on his paintings and was getting a lot done?" I asked. "He sounded like he was actually finishing paintings?"

"Well," Rita hummed, *"yes. I would have thought his studio would have at least a dozen or so paintings. But maybe his health kept him from being productive. Drinking again certainly would have. It did before."*

"Of course."

"He could have just been saying all that for my sake," Rita said, sadly. *"To make me not worry about what he was doing out there."*

"Right."

"Who knows with Prescott. He was always a big cagey."

"Makes sense," I said. "You didn't even know he had hired an assistant, after all."

Rita chuckled.

"That's true," she said. *"If he felt it was nobody's business, he wasn't going to tell anybody."*

I breathed out heavily, wondering why I'd bothered to call Rita Johnson. When she'd first picked up the phone, I found myself asking her questions I hadn't known I was thinking. My busybody nature had kicked in before I could stop it. Suddenly, I remembered the main purpose of my call.

"The main reason I called you today, Ms. Johnson," I said, "was to let you know we decided that—since there aren't any paintings—an as-is sale of the house and all contents is probably best. I'm sorry I don't have better news than that. However, I've turned everything over to Charlene. I'm sure she'll keep in touch with you and keep you in the loop about what the next steps are and all of that stuff."

Rita sighed.

"*It is what it is, isn't it?*" she asked. "*The house is nice enough. I'm sure it will sell for a pretty penny.*"

"I expect as much," I said. "It won't be as much as a ton of Prescott Pemberton paintings, but it won't be anything to spit on."

She chuckled again.

"*Thank you again, Jackson,*" she said. "*I appreciate all that you—and Charlene—have done for us.*"

"Of course," I said, ready to hang up the phone.

Suddenly, another thought struck me. Something Marv had said entered my head and I wasn't certain he had mentioned it to Ms. Johnson.

"Rita," I said, "do you remember when I asked you about Marshelle? Prescott's assistant?"

"*Of course.*"

"I had the wrong last name. She had told me it was Martin," I said. "But that was just a stage name or something she used in New York."

"*Oh?*"

"Yeah," I said. "Her real last name was Biggerstaff. Does Marshelle *Biggerstaff* ring a bell?"

Again, Rita was hemming and hawing on the other line. I knew I had plowed into another dead end with Ms. Rita Johnson.

"*Well,*" Rita said, "*no.*"

I sighed.

"*Not* Marshelle *Biggerstaff,*" she said. "*But that's the last name of that boy Prescott was seeing up here.*"

I sat up straight on the stool behind the counter.

"I'm sorry?"

"*Oh,*" Rita mumbled, "*you know. Prescott was...*"

"Got it," I said.

I didn't bother telling Rita that I belonged to the same tribe so there was no point in tip-toeing around the subject.

"*He was seeing some boy—I say 'boy' because he was in his twenties. Prescott never had any sense when it came to love. Anyway, that was that boy's last name.*"

I sat there, eyes unfocused, thinking hard as Rita talked.

"*Between you and me, that's when all of Prescott's troubles started. With that boy. Horrible little creature. Needy. Bratty. Mean. That's when Prescott started getting all his headaches and dizzy spells. That's what drove him to drink. That's my opinion anyway. I was so glad when he kicked that boy to the curb. And I was extra glad to see him get away from New York for a while. New York and that boy.*"

My eyes refocused and I felt my breath catch in my throat.

"*Are you still there?*" Rita asked.

"Yeah—yes," I stammered. "I'm sorry, Ms. Johnson. I have to go."

Rita Johnson was saying her goodbyes when I hung up the phone. Methodically, I grabbed my keys, my jacket, and exited the shop, locking the door tightly behind me.

CHAPTER TWENTY-TWO

It felt like I was knocking forever before Jeremy opened his front door. He was in basketball shorts and a t-shirt, his golden curls sticking up every which way like freshly mowed hay. Or a briar patch. When his eyes focused on who was standing in front of him, his look of curiosity switched to a scowl of annoyance. I couldn't blame him. However, the look wasn't going to scare me away.

"Can I come in?" I asked.

"What do you want, Jacks?" he asked, not opening the door wider.

"I want to talk to you," I said. "Can I come in?"

Jeremy opened the door a little wider, but placed his body directly in the gap, blocking me from entering his house. He crossed his arms over his chest and stared at me blankly, Obviously, he was still raw about all the things I'd said over the last few days. Whether the things I'd said had merit or not, or the questions I asked valid or not, he was still upset.

"So you can insult me some more?" he asked.

"So I can ask you some questions," I said.

He snorted derisively at me, and I couldn't blame him.

"So, basically, yes. You want to come in and insult me some more?"

"Jeremy," I said, "can I please come inside?"

He stared at me a moment longer, considering his options, but he finally let the door swing wide and stepped back, giving me access to his dark house. Reluctantly, I stepped inside, ducking into the shadows of the house. Obviously, my knocking had woken him up. He had probably been sleeping for another night shift—or had finished one that morning and was catching up on his rest. All the lights were still off and the house was quiet.

Jeremy gently shut the door, the latch clicking, which caused me to jump and turn to stare at him. He gave me an odd look, so I moved further into the living room. Following me, a frown on his face, Jeremy seemed perplexed instead of angry. Of course, my body language probably left a lot to be desired. I couldn't help it. I knew I was in danger.

But Jeremy and I had to talk.

Once I'd moved to the center of the living room, making sure I wasn't blocked in or backed up against anything, I turned to Jeremy.

"Have you talked to Marv today?" I asked.

Jeremy shook his head. "I've been in bed since I got home this morning. Why?"

Against my will, my head was turning, taking in the dark house around me, as though the bogeyman would jump out at any moment.

"Why, Jacks?" Jeremy asked sternly.

I jerked back to attention.

"Someone broke into my shop last night," I said. "Tried to stab me with my own butcher knife. Kind of scary. And humiliating."

Jeremy's eyes grew wide.

"Marv didn't tell me," Jeremy said. "Are you okay, Jacks?"

"I'm fine," I said, waving him off, though the hairs on the back of my neck were sticking up, prickly on my flesh. "I didn't call it in until this morning—you were probably already off shift."

He frowned at me.

"Why would you wait until this morning to call 911?" Jeremy growled. "Are you crazy? You could have been hurt? What if they came back?"

"I didn't want to tell Marv too much," I said.

Jeremy cocked his head to the side.

"Until I talked to you," I said.

"Why did you need to talk to me first?"

"See," I said, "the person didn't actually *break into* the shop. They let themselves inside. They had a key."

Jeremy stared at me quizzically for a moment, then a blush started to crawl up his cheeks.

"Besides me, only one other person has a key to the shop," I said. "You."

"Just great, Jacks," he said. "Just great. Now you're accusing me of…of…what? Coming to your shop to murder you? Do you know how crazy you sound? You've sounded insane for days, but this is really over the top."

I was shaking my head before he could finish his thought.

"No," I said. "That's not what I'm saying. I'm saying your key was used to get into my shop. But it couldn't have been you who used it. The person who used it didn't know to close the light switch box to keep Rattlesnatches from turning the lights back on. But I know who used your key."

Jeremy was shaking his head then.

"No one has been using my keys, Jacks," he said. "I *never* let anyone have my keys. I'm more responsible than that. Especially since I have keys to other people's property."

"I believe you," I said. And I did believe Jeremy. "You'd never loan your keys out to someone else. But sometimes you leave them at home, don't you?"

Jeremy started to say something, looked confused, and shut his mouth.

"Is your...*friend* here?" I asked, looking around again. "*Bobby*, was it?"

"Bob—what are you getting at, Jacks? Why do you want to talk to Bobby?"

Right as Jeremy said his name, Bobby stepped out of the kitchen to stand in the doorway into the living room. Like Jeremy, he was wearing basketball shorts and a t-shirt. Obviously, he had recently gotten out of bed as well. When my eyes flitted over Jeremy's shoulder, Jeremy caught the motion and turned his head.

"Bobby?" I asked.

"That's me," he said, a sneer on his face.

Obviously, he had heard everything I'd said to Jeremy.

He looked exactly as I remembered from the night Deb had pointed him out at Harper's.

"Bobby—," I said, and stopped myself. "*Robert* Biggerstaff?"

"*Robert...?*" Jeremy mumbled.

Before he could barely get the word out, Robert's hand came up. The flash of the knife glinted in my eye as he lunged past Jeremy, the tip of the blade aimed right at my chest. Tumbling backwards, I fell into the couch, watching as Bobby—and the knife—came right at me. Clenching my eyes shut, I didn't want to see the knife plunge into my chest when he reached me. However, the sharp sting of death never came, and I was sitting there, my eyes shut tightly for a few seconds, before I finally opened my eyes again.

Jeremy had gotten ahold of Bobby's wrist and pried the knife out of his hand. He was glaring at Bobby, snarling angrily in his face as he held him tightly, keeping him away from me. Then he grabbed Bobby's other wrist and twisted both his arms behind his back. Clutching my chest—not simply to make sure it wasn't bleeding—I breathed a sigh of relief.

"Jacks," Jeremy grunted, struggling with the angry Bobby, "go get my cuffs off my dresser. They're by my wallet. And keys."

CHAPTER TWENTY-THREE

Ultimately, the bookstore didn't get reopened after lunch. After nearly getting stabbed by Bobby at Jeremy's place, then helping place him under arrest, I figured giving a statement to the police was more important than reopening the store for the rest of the day. I was sitting in the police department at Marv's desk, sipping a cup of coffee so strong a spoon would stand up in it. Exactly how I liked it.

Eleven Prescott Pemberton paintings were stacked atop Marv's desk, a white towel stuck between each one for padding. I desperately wanted to find some cardboard to put between them instead of the towels. I wasn't certain that the white towels from the Inn would damage the paintings, but I figured it wasn't doing them any good, either.

After Jeremy had brought Bobby in to the station and told Marv what had happened, they immediately booked him for assault with a deadly weapon—*pending further charges*—and threw him in a cell. After I told Marv what he might find at the Inn, where Bobby was staying when he wasn't hanging out with Jeremy, Marv was able to get a search warrant based on the current charges.

Though it was likely Marv and Jeremy could have searched Bobby's room at the Inn without a warrant—as long as Lila Westbrook had given them permission—they wanted to cover their bases. Letting a suspect in a double homicide investigation get away scot-free due to a technicality would have been a major flub.

Aside from the missing Prescott Pemberton paintings, Jeremy and Marv found some of Marshelle Biggerstaff's belongings. Which had required a second warrant to cover all bases. Obviously, Bobby hadn't had time to get rid of all of the things he'd taken from her car. Additionally, they found a bag of soiled clothing that smelled remarkably fishy. However, the paintings were the most important find.

"Let's go through this," Marv said, appearing out of nowhere to slide into his desk chair across from me.

Jeremy sidled up to the side of Marv's desk and sat down on the edge, turning his body to watch me. Though he was behind me, so I couldn't see him, I heard Officer Riley slide into an empty chair to listen in on our conversation. I looked at Marv and Jeremy and sipped my coffee.

"You knew Bobby was the killer because…Jeremy had a key to your shop?" Marv asked. "A key you didn't tell me about this morning. Even though I specifically asked you about any extra keys."

I smiled awkwardly.

Marv shook his head, but he couldn't hide his smile.

"Not just because Jeremy had the only other key," I said, glancing at Jeremy. "But I talked to Rita Johnson—Prescott's sister?—before I went to Jeremy's. I told her Marshelle's real last name, but she still had no idea who Marshelle was. But she said she knew the last name because that was the last name of the guy Prescott was seeing in New York. A real dirt bag, apparently."

I glanced at Jeremy. He blushed and looked to Marv to avoid my eyes.

"You mentioned that Marshelle had a brother named Robert but you couldn't reach him at his place in New York," I said. "Deb pointed out *Bobby* the other night—though she called him *Billy*—at Harper's. Said it was the guy Jeremy was seeing. Then I remembered that Jeremy had been seeing Bobby for a few weeks now. Which coincided with when Prescott's medical problems returned full force."

Jeremy and Marv exchanged a look, then turned their attention back to me. I guzzled the last of my coffee—it was nearly room temperature anyway—and put the cup on the desk. Marv gestured at the cup and I waved him off. I'd had enough.

"So," I began, sitting back, "famous and rich Prescott Pemberton is in New York. Painting, selling paintings, getting accolades, on top of the world. Doing good for himself. If things go as planned, the boat keeps its course, he's going to retire by the time he's fifty-five with a ton of money and his choice of what to do with it."

Marv and Jeremy nodded along.

"But he meets Bobby. *Robert Biggerstaff.* A real piece of work. I don't know the specifics—Rita didn't tell me—but I get the feeling he was demanding, needy, verbally and emotionally abusive, and was probably using Prescott for his money. The stress probably led to Prescott drinking. If he ever was a drinker to begin with. I'm not so certain I believe that Prescott ever was an actual alcoholic."

Once again, Jeremy and Marv were frowning at each other.

"Then," I chewed at my lip, thinking through the next part since I was still piecing things together, "Prescott starts experiencing strange health problems. Could be stress from his work. From dating a piece of work like Robert Biggerstaff. Could be a lot of things."

"Well, what was it?" Marv snorted. "You a doctor now, too?"

Jeremy and I laughed.

"Aniline," I said, nodding firmly.

Jeremy and Marv looked at each, then at me, then said simultaneously, "*Aniline?*"

Nodding, I said, "Aniline is a chemical that has a lot of purposes. It's used in dyes, leathers, lots of things. But it's incredibly toxic. Skin contact is toxic and it's incredibly toxic if inhaled for a period of time. You can kill someone with it pretty easily if you know what you're doing. If not, you'll at least make them pretty sick. I'm guessing that Bobby—Robert—*whatever you want to call him*—was using aniline to try and kill Prescott."

"But why?" Marv asked. "What purpose did that serve?"

"To take any paintings he had," I said. "It's hard to prove a famous painter you're dating didn't gift you a bunch of his paintings if he's not alive to deny it, is it? And a famous painter's work is worth so much more after they're dead."

Jeremy frowned when I looked over at him.

"So," I continued quickly, "he was slowly poisoning Prescott. Fortunately, he was really bad at it, and Prescott got tired of putting up with him before he could finish the job. He ditched him, told him to never speak to him again, and moved back home to Head Rock Harbor to do his work. But not before hiring an assistant."

"Marshelle Martin," Jeremy said, smiling.

"At least, that's the name she gave him," I said, nodding. "When it was obvious that Bobby couldn't finish the job on his own, he convinced Marshelle to step in. She got the assistant job, came out here with Prescott, and, after gaining his trust, started trying to off him as well. Unfortunately, she didn't have the killer instinct like Bobby. She found it hard to poison another human being. Rita said her brother only had headaches and dizziness once a month or so once he got back to Head Rock Harbor—which tells me Marshelle couldn't bring herself to really commit to the job. But she was doing enough to make him concerned and lose his head from time to time. Which is probably why you had to go up there and talk to him those times, Marv. And every time she called you, that strengthened the alcoholic narrative—that's important for later. Between the aniline making some of his health problems return periodically and the stress he was under to recover and work hard on his paintings, he was probably a little out of touch with reality from time to time. However, Prescott was painting away, getting some of his best work done—"

I nodded at the stack of paintings.

"—and Bobby was back in New York, losing his patience," I said. "So, a few weeks ago, he came to town. He concocted a plan with Marshelle that he would help her finish the poisoning. But, and this is just an assumption, Bobby got a little 'hands on' when he attempted to finish the job. He didn't just slip some aniline in a drink or put it in a room humidifier, he got up close and personal with it. After all of his waiting, he was furious and, when Marshelle let him into the Pemberton place the night Prescott died, he simply attacked Prescott in his studio with the bottle of aniline. Probably threw it in his face or something. He probably had to act quickly since Prescott would have been shocked and panicked to see him."

Jeremy and Marv were leaning in as I spoke.

"Prescott ripped off his clothes and ran. Ran like he was out of his entire mind—because he was. The aniline was doing a number on him and he'd just been attacked by the crazy ex-boyfriend he'd hoped to never see again. Bobby grabbed one of the white towels in the studio, soaked it in aniline, and ran after, planning to smother him with it. That would account for the rash on Prescott's face that was mentioned in the autopsy report. They chased each other all the way down to the harbor. By that time, Bobby was tired of trying to do things the easy way."

"*This was easy?*" Jeremy mumbled.

I grinned and continued.

"So," I said, "he pulled the flood gauge up and beaned Prescott over the head with it. I found it stuck under the ramp the other day. I thought nothing of it at the time and put it back in place. But in Prescott's autopsy report, it said white paint chips were in his head wound. The flood gauge is painted white. Anyway, Prescott was dead when he hit the ground. Mavis Attberry said she saw ghosts after Prescott— at least that's what she told me. And I'm certain some naked guy running around in the dark with a white towel flapping around probably looked like ghosts to a drunk woman."

Marv snorted.

"Bobby left Prescott's body in the harbor and raced back to his room at the Inn, grabbed some towels, went back to the Pemberton place, and stole some paintings. Probably after using those same towels to clean up the mess he'd made with the aniline. He simply threw Prescott's aniline soaked clothes in the bathroom for the time being. He came back for those later. In fact, I think he was at the house the same time I was there deodorizing the studio. Anyway, after offing Prescott in the Harbor, he went out and celebrated at Harper's like the psycho he is. Which is where he met Jeremy and found out about the extra painting he needed to steal to complete the set."

Jeremy's eyes grew wide.

"And," I continued, "I'm guessing Marshelle was supposed to wrap things up with police, give her key back, then pick Bobby up at the Inn, and they'd go back to New York together with all of Prescott's paintings. When the time was right, and everyone in the art scene found out about Prescott's death, his ex-boyfriend could announce he had a bunch of Prescott's old paintings he'd been gifted, and gee, he'd sure like to sell them off."

Marv was clucking his tongue.

"But when Marshelle went to pick up Bobby, he wanted to stick around. Tie up some loose ends. She probably threatened him because she was feeling guilty—as she had all along—and he couldn't risk her messing up his plan. She had to go."

I looked at Marv.

"You told me she'd been dead for twelve hours, right? Well, I'd seen her nearly forty-eight hours before," I said. "If she'd crashed leaving the Pemberton's that day, her time of death would have been different. That let me know the crash had been staged, especially since the lack of blood at the scene was suspicious."

"That's true," Marv said, nodding.

"Unfortunately, she lived long enough after the staged crash to stumble out of her car and tumble into the gully and die. And that mostly brings us up to date. Well, Bobby tried to kill me in my store last night. And then again at Jeremy's today. Because he knew I was figuring things out from being in the Pemberton place at the same time as me and from hearing me talk to Jeremy at the front door of his house."

"But how did you know aniline was involved?" Jeremy asked suddenly. "Where'd you get that from?"

I couldn't help but chuckle.

"The pipes," I said. "Hydrogen sulfide got into the pipes of houses and businesses making an awful rotten egg smell. I could smell it in some people's houses—like yours the other day, Germ. And I vaguely smelled it on Charlene the day they found Prescott. Obviously, her clothes had picked up the smell when she was at home. But I smelled another bad smell around town, too. Something...*fishy*."

Marv and Jeremy looked confused.

"Lila Westbrook was folding towels one day at the Inn. They smelled fishy. Prescott's studio actually smelled fishy, not like rotten eggs, but I didn't notice. I thought it was all the same smell. Sawyer Robison even said the smell made him feel lightheaded. When I saw a bottle of aniline in Prescott's studio the night I was deodorizing it, I began to put two and two together, especially since the studio smelled so much better after the stinky pile of clothes was gone from the bathroom."

"Wait, wait, wait," Marv shook his head, "why did nothing show up on the toxicology report?"

"That's the thing," I said, excitedly. "*Nothing* showed up on the report. Not even alcohol. And Jeremy even told me that Prescott smelled like alcohol when y'all found him. However, the autopsy report said he smelled *fishy*."

"Yeah?" Marv urged me on.

Jeremy looked confused.

"One, I'm sure that Prescott had some level of aniline in his body. Phenylamine, aminobenzene, or benzamine will need to be checked for, Marv."

He nodded at me.

"But a Medical Examiner isn't going to test for those things unless they have a reason to. Why would they? That's just odd, right? Who would think to test for such an usual chemical unless they have some idea that a person has been exposed to it?"

Jeremy nodded along.

"However, the aniline didn't kill him anyway. The blow to the head did. So, two, Marshelle and Bobby decided to go along with the narrative of Prescott being a sloppy drunk who took a naked stroll in the harbor, tripped, fell, and bonked himself out of existence. If anyone asked Marshelle about Prescott, she was supposed to repeat what an alcoholic he was—if that was ever true. And even if aniline was found in a toxicology report, there would be a million reasons why an artist would be exposed to it. Aniline exposure wouldn't raise any suspicions of murder. And I suspect Prescott smelled like alcohol because Bobby either came back and dumped some on him, or when Mavis tried to help Prescott, she spilled some on him. She was just too out of her gourd to realize he was beyond help."

Marv sat back and Jeremy smiled down at me.

"It was kind of perfect," I said. "Whether he was an alcoholic who fell and hit his head or he was a painter who got exposed to a chemical, both would be considered accidental deaths. They still had a dead painter's paintings to sell off at a later time."

"Well," Marv said, "I would ask you to explain how you know what was in the autopsy and toxicology reports—"

I grinned awkwardly.

"—but I'm just glad we have this solved," Marv said. "Just one question, if you'll indulge me?"

"Sure," I said with a shrug.

"Why didn't Bobby leave when the getting was good?" Marv asked. "You said it was set up perfectly so that no matter what the Medical Examiner said was the cause of death that murder wouldn't be suspected. So, why stick around to tie up loose ends?"

Chewing at my lip, I glanced furtively at Jeremy, then back at Marv.

"Greed," I said.

"Greed?" Marv asked.

"You have eleven paintings there," I said. "*The Months of Head Rock Harbor*."

Marv nodded, then a lightbulb went off over his head.

"There should be twelve," he said quickly.

Nodding, I said, "Bobby was devising a plan to steal the twelfth one. Well, actually, the first one. To complete the set. Even if he had to commit another murder. The whole set would sell for so much more than selling them off one at a time."

Jeremy was suddenly looking down at his lap. Out of the corner of my eye, I could see him fidget. Marv was frowning at me.

"But where's the final painting?" he asked.

I didn't look at Jeremy, but I didn't answer Marv, either. Finally, Jeremy sighed and turned to look at his chief.

"It's hanging on my living room wall," he said. "Prescott gave it to me nine months ago."

Marv stared at Jeremy for the longest time until Jeremy was looking at his lap again.

"Jackson," Marv said, "I need you to give us privacy to talk about this final painting, Jeremy's affiliation with the suspect *and* victim, and how his keys have been used by the suspect to enter other people's property."

"Sure," I said softly.

Even though I hadn't wanted to do it, and I'd done everything to avoid it, I'd still sold Jeremy up the river. However, at least I'd proved that he wasn't the one who had killed Prescott or attempted to murder me. I rose from the seat across from Marv and shuffled out of the office.

"I'll call you for an official interview date later, Jackson," Marv hollered after me.

"Okay," I replied softly over my shoulder.

Then I left the police department and made my way home in the late afternoon sun.

Cops. You solve their case and they don't even offer you a ride home.

CHAPTER TWENTY-FOUR

Sunday was a slow day around the bookstore. Since I never open on Sundays, even when I've missed half a Saturday the day before, I spent most of my day dusting shelves and straightening inventory. Rattlesnatches did his best to help by staying out of the way and supervising from atop the bookshelves, staring down at me as I worked. I wasn't certain if my work was quite up to his expectations, but he didn't meow at me too much.

Around mid-morning, I got a text from Deb, apologizing for her behavior the other night. *Will you forgive me?* She'd asked. *Like you always do?* After a moment, I texted back. *Yeah. Forgiven. Just give me a few days.* Wisely, she didn't respond. She let me go back to my life. So, I went back to my work of dusting and straightening the bookstore.

Though Sundays weren't inventory days and were really meant to be relaxation days, I still did a bit of inventory. Then I ate lunch, which consisted of the last of the leftovers in the fridge. A bit of casserole here, some roasted veggies, half a salad—I made a buffet out of all of the things I hadn't managed to eat in the last couple of days. Munchies would have been an okay option for lunch, but staying at home felt right.

I'd just sat down in the chair by the door into my apartment to begin working on the *Don't Let the Cat Out or the Cops In* cross-stitch when there was a knock on the front door. Groaning, I put the embroidery hoop in the basket with the skeins of thread and stood up so I could see the front door from the balcony. When I saw the mop of golden curls, then Jeremy looking up at me from outside, I smiled. He smiled back.

I went downstairs, Rattlesnatches following behind, and unlocked the front door. Jeremy stepped inside and shut the door behind himself, then locked the door once more.

"Hey, Jacks," he said.

"Hey yourself."

He sighed and reached up to rub the back of his neck.

"I really screwed up this time," he said. "Sleeping with the enemy and all that. Treating my best friend like garbage, and—"

I didn't want to hear him whine. Not that I didn't care, but it was pointless.

"What did Marv say?" I asked, interjecting. "Do you still have a job?"

Jeremy chuckled softly. "Yeah. I'm still a detective for Head Rock Harbor. But I'm missing half my rear end."

I chuckled. "Could be worse."

"I gave him the painting. He's going to make sure the family gets all twelve."

"It was a gift from Prescott," I said. "You came by it legally and ethically."

He shrugged. "Not telling him about it as soon as I knew Prescott was dead basically forfeited it. At least in my mind. And Marv's."

"Fair enough."

Jeremy slumped against the check-out counter and grinned tiredly at me.

"I just keep getting involved with the wrong men," he said.

Reaching out, I chucked him under the chin.

"You'll grow up one day, bud."

Smiling, he said, "Or I'll make an honest man out of you one day. Let you take me away from this wild and crazy life I live."

I rolled my eyes.

"That's asking too much of me," I said, snorting derisively, though I meant it to be playful.

Jeremy grinned at me. "Is it too much to ask for a Sunday dinner invitation?"

Rolling my eyes even harder, I shrugged.

"I guess I can throw something together for dinner tonight," I said. "But don't expect any miracles. I've been really busy solving double homicides and haven't gotten to the grocery store in ages."

Jeremy laughed.

"I could bring a pizza," he suggested. "If you want to avoid cooking for a night."

"It's a deal," I said.

"And then a movie after?" he asked. "Just the two of us?"

"Sounds good," I agreed. "I've got some work I need to do before dinner. So…let's say seven?"

"Works for me," Jeremy turned to head towards the front door. "What work? You starting another cross-stitch?"

The way Jeremy said "cross-stitch" always sounded derisive, but in a playful way. I nudged him in the shoulder as we approached the door, making him laugh.

"I was actually working on one when you showed up just now," I said. "But actually, I realized that I should really start on a project I've been putting off for a month or so. So, get a really good pizza to bring for dinner. I'll be hungry."

"All right," Jeremy chuckled as I unlocked and opened the door for him so he could step out of the shop.

"Hey," I said, making him turn to look at me. "I have something for you."

Jeremy watched as I dug in my pocket. I pulled my hand out, producing a key.

"New key to the new lock," I nodded at the door. "In case you need it."

Cautiously, Jeremy smiled as he took the key from my hand, not quite meeting my eyes.

"Thanks," he said. "Thanks, Jacks."

"I don't want to have to come downstairs to let you in every time you visit," I said with a shrug.

He smiled. "See you at seven?"

"It's a deal."

"It's a date," Jeremy said, shooting me a quick grin before dashing away.

My brow furrowed as I watched him race across the street to his cruiser, pull his own keys out of his pocket, and climb inside. He flashed me another smile and a wave from inside the vehicle, then pulled away from the curb, driving off towards the harbor. Shaking my head, I went back into the shop and locked the door behind me.

Back across the shop, I climbed the stairs once again. When I got to the balcony, I ignored my chair and the cross-stitch and went into my apartment. Rattlesnatches ran in after me and leapt onto the bed, immediately curling up into a ball and getting into nap mode. Chuckling at him, I pulled my laptop out from the bookshelf and went over to the kitchen table.

I sat down and opened the laptop, hitting the button to power it on. Cracking my knuckles, I waited for the laptop to power up. When it did, I opened a Word document and stared at it for a moment. Finally, an idea popped into my brain. Well, the ghost of an idea.

I typed:

An Artful Assault
A Detective Randy Melton Mystery
By Harrison Garner

Smiling down at the screen, I cracked my neck, stretched my arms, then put my fingers to the keys. Harrison Garner wasn't ready to hang up his hat yet. It was time to write another bestseller.

Keep reading for a sneak-peek at the first chapter of MURDER IN THE ROUGH (HEAD ROCK HARBOR MYSTERY #2) – due in 2024!

Chapter One

Sawyer's boat was typical for a regular citizen of Head Rock Harbor, meaning it was a basic 18-foot Jon boat with a 60-horsepower outboard motor for open water and a 24v trolling motor for the shallows. Unlike other boats in town, Sawyer had taken the time to install a padded high-back folding boat seat for himself at the back and had added vinyl-covered padding to all of the other bench seats. My tailbone was thanking him as we sliced through and bobbed on the choppy waters of Old Man River. The fact that he kept his boat clean and in immaculate condition had the fussy side of me thanking him as well.

"*Whoooooooooooop!*" Sawyer hooted as the boat crested and flopped over a particularly impressive wave.

As the bow slammed back onto the Mississippi, ice-cold water sprayed over the bow and spritzed my face. I pulled my jacket more tightly around myself. Thinking about having a face full of Mississippi water made my nose turn up. I shot a look over my shoulder at Sawyer and he laughed. It was late April, crawling towards May, but the water still felt like we'd just abandoned winter. The wind felt like pinpricks on my neck and face, especially when combined with the water spray from the river.

Fortunately, between the wind and the choppiness of the river, Sawyer finally realized that his joyful recklessness was leading to danger. He let up on the throttle and brought us down to a speed where we were slicing through the waves as opposed to hurdling them. My stomach grumbled as it settled back into its regular place in my gut.

"*Sorry!*" Sawyer shouted as the boat slowed, then reverted to a normal speaking voice once our speed evened out. "Just had to have a little fun."

"When you asked me to come with you, I thought it would be less stressful than avoiding Charlene," I said. "Now I see that I have chosen poorly."

Chuckling, Sawyer said, "Nah. It's fine. I was just excited to be back out on the river. I won't get you hurt, I swear."

"I'd appreciate it."

I reached up and ran my fingers through my brown curls, wondering how much I resembled a drowned rat. For being a resident of Head Rock Harbor, I'm not keen on the cult of the river. As a concept, it's nice. Walking along the shores and taking in the views, sitting and staring out at the passing boats, and catching sights of wildlife—that interests me. The water may be brown, but it's still somehow beautiful. However, the boat culture of Head Rock Harbor wasn't ingrained in my DNA as it was with most of the population.

Though I had absolutely nothing against my fellow Head Rock Harbor citizens who practically worshipped the river during the warmer months, I was more of a passive river lover. Though I'd never refer to myself as "outdoorsy," I also wouldn't call myself a strictly indoors type of guy, either. I enjoyed the outdoors. However, I preferred activities that kept me out of the muck and away from danger. A nice hike in the woods? Wonderful. Hurtling over waves of muddy water in an aluminum boat at thirty miles per hour? Not my cup of tea.

Then again, risking life and limb in an open-air tin coffin was preferable to church. Which was how I'd found myself in Sawyer's boat out on the Mississippi looking for illegal trot lines to cut. Charlene had accosted me on Saturday afternoon in the shop, informing me that she was taking me to church the next day, and then out to lunch. Apparently, we had *a lot to discuss* about the Harbor Street Business Owners Association. Since I was not a member, nor had I expressed any interest in being involved in the HSBOA, I had no idea what we could possibly have to discuss.

So, when Sawyer had texted that evening and asked if I wanted to go out on his boat with him the next day, I'd practically leapt at the opportunity. Staying at home, in my pajamas, and watching something trashy on T.V. while curled up in bed with Rattlesnatches would have been best. Forced to choose between church and the river—I took the river. Rattlesnatches and T.V. would be waiting once Sawyer took me back home. Whenever that time came.

"City Council told everyone to have their lines pulled by the fifteenth," Sawyer announced as he let up on the motor, the deafening roar suddenly a murmur. "But Marv says that people have been spotting plenty over the last few days."

"Why didn't Marv send Jeremy or Ashley to come out here and yank 'em?" I asked, turning to straddle the bench to talk now that it was safe.

"Don't take away my side hustles, man," Sawyer chuckled. "The city's paying me to come out here and cut these lines."

I laughed with him.

"I guess if you're dying to do it, I have no objections," I said.

"I saved you from church," Sawyer reminded me. "Show a little gratitude."

Chuckling, I gazed at the trees lining the shore as we puttered along the river. Even though I'd joined Sawyer on his boat to avoid Charlene, I was still expected to help. Two pairs of eyes looking out for the tell-tale signs of heavy fishing line leading out of the water was better than one. Even though trotlines use heavier fishing line than what you'd find on a fishing pole, it's still nearly invisible against the movement of the water and the camouflage of the trees and their wind-rustled leaves. With both Sawyer's and my eyes watching, we had a better chance of catching all of the illegal lines.

"So," I asked, "what happens if we find any?"

"We yank 'em up, check the snoods, free any fish, and pull up the lines to toss when we get back to town," Sawyer explained.

"How do we know who put the line out?"

"We don't." Sawyer sounded deflated. "That's the worst part."

"So, we don't get to give Marv names of people to give tickets to?" I asked, smiling over at Sawyer. "This is boring."

Sawyer chuckled, but I could see in his face that he agreed. Finding illegal trotlines that were set to catch fish after the allowed dates and having no one to punish was annoying. When people break the law—especially when it involves protecting animals—some form of punishment is best. Knowing people would get off without so much as a ticket was irksome. Then again, a lot of people fished to feed their families, so I found myself with an ethical conundrum.

I decided to push my feelings away and focus on finding the lines to cut.

We puttered along the river, ten yards from the shore for a while, our eyes focused on finding any lines. For a while, I figured we were simply wasting our time. When the City Council tells Marv to send someone out to cut illegal lines, word spreads quickly. It was possible that all of the people who had set lines had already harvested and cut the lines before we'd gotten on the river. However, the smallest flash of orange caught my eye suddenly.

"Got one!" I announced, pointing towards the shore.

Tied around the low-hanging branch of a cottonwood was the tiniest sliver of orange fabric. Next to it, a nearly invisible line ran down into the water. If it hadn't been for the person who set the line marking the spot to make it easier for them to find it, I wouldn't have known it was there. Fortunately, a fisherman making concessions for his poor memory landed me the first spotting of an illegal line.

"You lucked out," Sawyer said. "That one's tagged."

"Still in the lead," I replied. "'S'not my fault you missed it."

Grumbling playfully, Sawyer directed us toward the shallows. In the flat-bottomed Jon boat, it was easy for Sawyer to get us right up to the branch of the tree. He had to pull the motor up to keep from getting stuck in the viscous Mississippi mud. We'd probably have to use the oars to push back out into deeper water so we could put the motor back down. However, we didn't have to get out of the boat and get wet and muddy. That's all that mattered to me.

I watched as Sawyer grabbed the tree limb and used physical force to pull the boat into position next to the trotline. Working quickly, he used his pocketknife to snip the line, then deftly began pulling it into the boat. Every two to three feet, we'd find a snood—a smaller line hanging off the main line with a baited hook attached. Fortunately, even though the trotline was fairly long, none of the hooks had fish attached. Several had lost their bait—either to the water or clever fish—but none had caught anything.

"One down," Sawyer said.

He had curled the line up like a lasso by his feet and was readjusting himself in his seat.

"You want to pass me a beer?" he asked, pointing at the cooler next to my bench seat.

"Sure," I said.

I opened the Igloo Playmate cooler—an honest-to-goodness red and white Igloo Playmate cooler—and fetched a can of Pabst Blue Ribbon for Sawyer. Smiling, he caught the beer that I tossed him, and opened it immediately, ignoring the spritz of foam. Laughing at him, I pulled a soda out of the cooler and popped the tab.

"You're up," Sawyer said, nodding at the oars.

Groaning, I put my soda can between my knees, holding it tightly, and grabbed an oar. Leaning over a bit, I pushed the oar into the water next to us until I felt resistance, and pushed away from the mushy floor of the river. I held onto the oar handle like a vice since the mud did its best to suck it out of my grip. The boat drifted away from shore and I

230

yanked the oar out of the mud. I gave it a twirl in the water to rinse off, then pulled it back into the boat to lay alongside the hull once more.

Sawyer gave me an approving nod, then dropped the trolling motor once we had drifted out far enough. He started the motor up and we were puttering away again, sipping our drinks as we watched the trees on the shore like hawks.

Over the next hour, Sawyer found two more lines and I found one, keeping us tied in score and making us both search harder for trotlines. There was no prize for finding the most lines, but the competitive nature of us both kept the game exciting. By the time we were tied two to two, we were not speaking to each other, focusing solely on spotting lines. The game was afoot and we were playing as though our lives depended upon it.

Sawyer was on his third beer—*I had no intention of tattling to Marv*—and I was on my second soda when Sawyer spotted the fifth illegal trotline.

"*Whoooooooop!*" Sawyer hollered again.

Pumping one fist in the air, he finally pointed to the line that he spotted tied to a stake on the shore. We had been rounding a bend, an anabranch in the river, when he'd spotted the line.

"That's not fair," I demanded playfully. "We were coming around the bend."

"You're at the front of the boat, man!" Sawyer laughed, pointing out my advantage.

I merely shot him a smile over my shoulder, letting him know there were no hard feelings, and the trolling motor sputtered, easing us toward the shore. Sawyer was still chuckling, proud of his keen eyesight as he aimed us towards the shore. Seeing his chest puffed out so proudly made me want to grab a handful of ice from the cooler to chuck at him—*in a playful way, of course*—but I somehow managed to ignore the intrusive thought.

We were barely ten feet from the shore when the trolling motor sputtered and kicked, lifting out of the water. With an incredibly Midwestern "ope," Sawyer caught it, switching it off as he simultaneously nestled it in the upright position out of the water. A second later, the bow of the boat bumped into the muddy bottom of the river and the boat shuddered.

"I'm not getting in the mud," I said immediately.

Sawyer laughed.

"Seriously," I said. "You're getting paid for this. Not me."

I joined him in laughing.

"Well," Sawyer said, reaching up to rub his chin, "we're not that far out. And the riverbed is mush right up to the shore right now. The water's probably just high enough. We can probably use the oars to push up to the shore and hop out onto dry land. Then we can push away with the oars after we get the line pulled up."

"Sounds reasonable," I said, reaching for an oar. "I need to answer Mother Nature's call anyway."

"Agreed," Sawyer burped. "The PBRs are doing their job."

"Classy," I said.

Laughing, Sawyer grabbed the other oar. In unison, me on the right and him on the left, we pushed the oars through the shallow water, down into the riverbed, and pushed towards shore. When the bow of the Jon boat bumped the shore, it got lodged into the mud enough to keep us from floating away. Sawyer and I pulled the oars back into the boat and scrambled carefully out of the boat onto shore.

Before addressing the trotline or the call of nature, Sawyer tied the boat off on a nearby tree limb. With the boat in the shallows and the mud cradling its bottom, it was unlikely to drift away. However, the possibility was undesirable enough that precautions had to be taken. I waited patiently for Sawyer to secure the boat, stretching my arms and legs at his side.

"That should do it," he said. "If you want to go take care of business, I'll take care of the trotline first."

"Sounds good." I agreed.

Turning to walk away from Sawyer, I got a sudden flash of an idea of where we were on the river.

"Hey," I turned back to Sawyer, "is that the Wilford Woods?"

Jabbing a thumb over my shoulder towards the woods off from the shore, Sawyer turned to look where I was pointing. He squinted his eyes and considered my question for a moment, then nodded.

"You're right," Sawyer said.

"Jeremy and I used to hike the trail through there all the time back in high school," I said. "Opens out right behind the trailer park."

"Well," Sawyer laughed, "I'd rather use the boat. That's a good five miles from here and I don't think I have the hike in me after three beers."

I agreed with a chuckle. Silently, I stepped away and left Sawyer to deal with the trotline. I didn't have to go far to find a large tree for privacy. The woods were a mere ten yards away from the shore. Quickly, I set about doing my business. Once done and decent again, I moved away from the tree and turned to head back to meet Sawyer at the shore.

As I was turning, a flash of orange caught my eye, and I stopped and stared into the woods. How I'd missed it walking over to the tree, I couldn't figure, but the bright orange fabric deeper in the woods was obviously a tent. Frowning, I stared into the woods at the tent out in the middle of nowhere.

It wasn't uncommon for people to camp out in Wilford Woods, a secluded area at the south end of town. Jeremy and I had camped a few times back in our school days. It was close enough to town that if we had an emergency, one of us could run for help quickly, but it was far enough away that it felt like we were kind of roughing it. However, since there was a trotline staked into the shore, I had to wonder if the person camping twenty yards away was the owner.

"Got the line pulled up," Sawyer's voice a few feet behind me made me jump. "Two fish. Got 'em thrown back."

Spinning to find Sawyer grinning at my jumpy reaction, I jabbed a thumb over my shoulder.

"Someone's camping out here," I said.

Squinting, Sawyer leaned to look over my shoulder.

"Looks like it," he said with a nod. "Probably the jackwagon that put the trotline out."

I nodded. "That's what I'm thinking."

Shaking his head, Sawyer moved to put his back to me and sidled up to the tree.

"Let me answer this call and we'll go check it out," he said.

"All right."

I turned my back to give Sawyer privacy and stared out into the woods at the neon orange tent peeking out between the trees. No smoke was rising from the area of the campsite and I didn't hear any voices drifting through the woods. Of course, the woods were dense so it was possible that if the campers were being quiet, we wouldn't hear them out by the shore. Other than the tent I couldn't see any signs of life, though.

Typically, you'd see people moving around a campsite, smoke rising from a fire, voices of people talking and having a good time, and maybe some music if the campers were fancy. However, the woods were quiet. All I could hear was the sound of Sawyer answering Mother Nature's call behind me. When I heard the tell-tale zipping sound, signaling that he was done, I turned back to face him.

"Well," he said, pulling his shirt down over the front of his jeans, "should we go check it out?"

I shrugged.

"I don't know," I said. "I don't see anyone out there. And if they don't care about fishing laws, they're probably not going to be super happy if we show up to chew them out about it."

Sawyer thought about that for a moment.

"We don't know how many people might be out here." He agreed.

"Right."

"It's probably local kids," he said with finality, then pushed away from the tree. "Let's go give them a scare. Make 'em think they're getting in big trouble."

Sawyer's devilish grin made me chuckle and I fell into step beside him warily.

"But if it's not," I began, hustling alongside him, "and it's some guy out here with a bunch of guns, I'm going to be really mad at you if we get shot."

Sawyer laughed as we began to walk through the woods. After a few yards through the growth, Sawyer leaned his head back and hollered.

"*Anyone out here?*" he bellowed.

We continued to stomp through the brush, dodging tree limbs as we made our way closer to the orange tent and the campsite. I had expected to hear a voice holler back at us, or at least see a head poke up through the trees, searching for the source of Sawyer's voice. However, the campsite remained still and quiet as a churchyard as we approached. Sawyer shot me a glance and a shrug, which I returned.

Moments later, we were pushing through the last bit of brush and stepping into the small clearing in the woods where the unknown campers had set up. Though obviously having been in use, the campsite was presently unoccupied. The flaps at the opening were tied back and a quick glance inside the tent showed it to be empty.

Though I didn't want to disrupt other people's belongings, I pushed back the flap of the tent to get a better look into the tent. Everything seemed in place for a campsite. A sleeping bag set up that could accommodate two people at most, a little table with a battery-operated lantern, a bag that probably contained fresh clothes and toiletries—the usual camping accouterments. Nothing out of the usual, but nobody was inside of the tent.

Around the campsite, it looked as though a fresh fire hadn't been lit recently. The firepit was full of sashes and when I knelt to put my hand near the center, no warmth radiated from it. No lingering smoldering embers flickered. A folding chair was set near the firepit, facing it, and a large chest cooler was alongside the chair. It was either for easy access to drinks or for the dual function of also providing additional seating. That made it impossible to tell how many people had been, or were, using the campsite.

"No one here," Sawyer said.

I made a non-committal sound with my throat. The two of us looked around the clearing, but it was futile. No one was

"They probably went for a hike. Or maybe they are out on their boat?" Sawyer suggested.

Nodding along, it was possible the camper—or campers—had gone for a hike through the woods. It was also possible they had come to the campsite by boat and were currently out enjoying the river. Whatever the case, there was no one to ask about the illegal trotline at the moment. However, if they had come to the campsite by boat, it made it more likely that they had set the trotline.

"I think that—"

Before I could finish my thought, my wandering eyes fell on a pair of boots sticking out from behind a tree at the edge of the campsite. Frowning, I wondered why anyone would set their boots so far away from the tent.

"What?" Sawyer asked.

Not responding verbally, I gestured for him to follow me. Sawyer fell in step behind me as I crossed the campsite, walking the few yards between the tent and the tree.

"What are those doing there?" Sawyer asked as we approached the tree. "That's a weird spot to put boots."

When we rounded the tree, there was no need to give my take on the strange spot where the boots had been left. Because there were a pair of legs coming out of the boots. Most importantly, there was a whole body attached to those legs. And that body was staring up at the trees above, lifeless and unseeing. The obvious shotgun blast chest wound and blood-stained shirt of the man told us all we needed to know.

Wind whistled through the campsite as Sawyer and I stared down at the dead body.

"You get the credit for finding this trotline," Sawyer said quietly.

About the Author

Chase Connor spends his days writing about the people who live (loudly and rent-free) in his head when he's not busy being enthusiastic about naps and Pad Thai. Chase started his writing career as a confused gay teen looking for an escape from reality. Ten years later, one of the books he wrote during those years, *Just A Dumb Surfer Dude: A Gay Coming-of-Age Tale*, was published independently. Chase has numerous projects in various stages of completion lined up for publishing. Chase is a multi-genre author, but always with a healthy dollop of gay.

Chase can be reached at
chaseconnor@chaseconnor.com
Or on Twitter @ChaseConnor7
On Bluesky as chaseconnorbooks
He can also be found on his website Chase Connor Books
or on Goodreads

SIGN UP FOR THE CHASE CONNOR BOOKS NEWSLETTER AT CHASECONNOR.COM

He does his very best to respond to all DMs, emails, and Twitter comments from his reader-friends and loves the interaction with them. Chase has several novellas/novels for sale in e-book, paperback, hardback, and audiobook formats wherever books are sold.

www.ingramcontent.com/pod-product-compliance
Lightning Source LLC
Chambersburg PA
CBHW030136180626
46812CB00002B/708